Also Available in Norton Paperback Fiction

THE
FIREMAN'S WIFE

AND OTHER STORIES

Richard Bausch

W.W. NORTON & COMPANY
NEW YORK   LONDON

Printed in the United States of America.

Several of these stories have appeared in the following magazines:
"The Fireman's Wife" and "Luck" in *The Atlantic Monthly*; "Letter to the
Lady of the House" and "Consolation" in *The New Yorker*; "The Eyes of
Love" in *Esquire*; "Design" (under the title "A Kind of Simple, Happy
Grace") in *Wig Wag*. The story "Old West" was first published
in slightly different form in *Louder Than Words*, an anthology of
donated short stories brought out by Vintage Press, the proceeds
of which go toward fighting homelessness and illiteracy.

Library of Congress Cataloging in Publication Data

Bausch, Richard, 1945–
The fireman's wife and other stories/Richard Bausch.
p.   cm.
I. Title.
PS3552.A846F5   1991
813'.54—dc20   91–18415

ISBN 0-393-30790-5
W. W. Norton & Company, Inc.
500 Fifth Avenue, New York, N.Y. 10110
W. W. Norton & Company, Ltd.
10 Coptic Street, London WC1A 1PU

2   3   4   5   6   7   8   9   0

For Karen again,
*   and for our children:*
*   Wesley, Emily, Paul, Maggie, Amanda*

". . . Happy love, more happy, happy love!"

—KEATS

CONTENTS

WEDLOCK

HONEYMOON night, Howard locked the motel room door, flopped down on the bed and, clasping his hands behind his head, regarded her for a moment. He was drunk. They were both drunk. They had come from the Starlight Room, where they had danced and had too much champagne. They had charmed the desk clerk, earlier, with their teasing and their radiant, happy faces. The desk clerk was a woman in her mid-fifties, who claimed a happy, romantic marriage herself.

"Thirty-five years and two months," she'd said, beaming.

"Not even thirty-five hours," Howard had said. His face when he was excited looked just like a little boy's. "But it's not Lisa's first one."

"No," Lisa said, embarrassed. "I was married before."

"Well, it's this one that counts," the desk clerk had said.

Lisa, twenty-five years old, three years older than her new husband, had felt vaguely sorry to have the woman know this rather intimate detail about her past. She was nervous about it; it felt like something that wasn't cleared up, quite, though she hadn't seen Dorsey in at least two years—hadn't seen him in person, that is. He had called that once, and she'd told Howard about it. She'd complained to Howard about it, and even so had felt weirdly as if she were telling lies to him. Many times over the weeks of her going with Howard she'd wished the first marriage had never happened, for all her talk with her friends at work about what an experience it was, being married to a rock-'n'-roll singer and traveling around the country in that miserable van, with no air-conditioning and no windows.

Somehow she'd kept her sense of humor about the whole bad three years.

And tonight she'd made Howard laugh, talking about being on the road, traipsing from one motel to another and riding all those miles in a bus with people she wouldn't cross the sidewalk to see; it was astonishing how quickly dislikes and tensions came out in those circumstances. You just went from place to place and smiled and performed and shook hands and hung around and you hated everybody you were with most of the time, and they hated you back. It was worse, and somehow more intimate, than hatred between family members because for one thing you didn't hold back the stuff that scraped the raw places; you didn't feel compelled to keep from hitting someone in the sweet spot, as she liked to call it. You just went ahead and hit somebody's weakest point, and you kept hitting it until you drew blood. She'd kept on about it because he was staring at her with his boy's eyes, all dreamy and half drunk, and finally they were both laughing, both potted, feeling goofy and special and romantic, like the couple in the happy end of a movie, walking arm in arm down the long corridor of the motel to their room. They had come stumbling in, still holding on to each other, and finally Howard had lurched toward the bed and dropped there.

Where he now crossed his ankles and smiled at her, murmuring, "So."

She said, "So."

"Nobody knows where we are."

"Right," she said.

"We're—" he made a broad gesture. "Hidden away."

"Hidden away," she said.

"Just the two of us."

"Just us, right."

"Strip," he said.

She looked at him, looked into his innocent, chilly blue eyes.

"Want to play a game?"

"A game," she said.

"Let's play charades."

"Okay."

"You start," he said.

"No, you start."

"I'm really sick of starting all the time," he said. "I start the car and I start—" he seemed confused. "The car."

They laughed.

He got up and went to the bathroom door. "I know—wait a minute. I'll come out and you tell me who I am."

She waited. He staggered through the door. He was a very funny, very good-natured young man. It was what she loved about him.

"Here I come," he sang.

She sang back, "I'm ready when you are."

When he danced out of the bathroom, he lost his balance and stumbled onto the bed. As he bounced there, she laughed, holding her sides and leaning against the door.

"One more time," he said, then paused and put one finger over his lips. "Shhhhh. It's necessary to be very quiet."

She said, " Right. Shhhh."

"I don't guess you could tell who it was from the first time."

She shook her head. She was laughing too hard to speak. "Sure?"

"Stumbly?" she said.

"Stumbly."

"Isn't that one of the Seven Dwarfs?"

"Stumbly," he said, looking around. He seemed out of breath, but of course it was the champagne. "Hey, how do I know? I never even met Sleeping Beauty."

"Snow White," she said.

He said, "Right," and threw himself onto the bed, bouncing again, lying flat on his back with his legs and arms outspread. She let herself slide down against the door, and her dizziness felt good, as though she were floating in deep space, held up by clouds.

He'd come off the bed. "Okay, let's try again."

"Snow White," she said.

He laughed. "Now watch. You'll know who it is."

Again he went into the bathroom.

"I'm ready," she said.

He peeked out at her, held one finger to his lips again. "Shhhh."

"Shhhh," she said.

Once more he was gone. She made herself comfortable against the door, letting her legs out and folding her arms. It seemed to her now that in all the three years with Dorsey she had never had such a lighthearted time. Everything with Dorsey had been freighted with his drive to make it big, his determination to live out some daydream he'd had when he was thirteen. Married to him, traveling with him, watching him pretend to be single and listening to him complain at night about bad bookings, stupid sidemen, the road, and the teen hops where kids asked over and over for the cheap radio stuff—living with all this, she had never felt the kind of uncomplicated pleasure-in-the-moment that she had experienced from the beginning with Howard, who was quite unlike Dorsey in all the important ways. Oddly enough, for all Dorsey's rock-band outrageousness and all his talk of personal freedom, she felt much less constrained around Howard, who was a plumber's apprentice and had no musical or artistic talent whatsoever. From the beginning, she'd felt comfortable with him, as though he were a younger brother she'd grown up with. The fact that he *was* younger wasn't as important, finally, as the fact that he made her feel like laughing all the time, and was wonderfully devoid of the kinds of anxiety that always plagued Dorsey. Worries about health, about the world situation, the environment, the future. The trouble, finally, was that Dorsey had never learned how to have fun, how to let go and just see what happened.

Dorsey would never have allowed this, for instance, getting tight and being a sort of spectacle to the other guests at the hotel. She remembered that Howard had stopped someone in the hall—a squat-looking, balding man in a blue bathing suit with a towel wrapped around his neck and shower clogs under one arm—and, with a voice soaked in portent, announced that all the moons were unfavorable. Somehow he'd managed it with such good-natured goofiness that the man had simply smiled and walked on.

"HEY," she said now. "What're you doing in there?"

"I'm transforming," he said. "You won't believe it."

"I'm getting sleepy."

"Guess who this is," he said.

"I'm waiting."

When he came out this time, he had removed his shirt, and his shoes and socks. He came slowly, bending down to peer in all directions, looking very suspicious and wary. "Well?" he said, barely able to keep his feet.

"I don't know. Not Stumbly?"

"No," he said. "Look close." And he paraded past her again.

"God, I can't get it."

"Groucho. Ever see him walk? Groucho Marx. Look."

"Oh."

"Okay," he said, smiling, straightening with exaggerated dignity. "I'd like to see you try it."

"I want to see you do Stumbly again."

"Hey," he said. "You think your mother likes me as much as she liked old Dorsey?"

"Better," she said.

"Can't understand how a lady could like somebody like that."

"She liked his hands," Lisa said. "Isn't that silly? I think that's just so silly. She liked his beautiful hands."

"Do I have beautiful hands?" he wanted to know.

"Beautiful," she said.

"Okay. Try this one." He lurched into the bathroom again.

"Howard?" she said. "My mother likes you a lot."

"She thinks you're robbing the cradle."

"Oh, don't be ridiculous."

"True."

"That's just dumb. If anything, she's jealous."

"Of my hands?"

"I think she likes your tush, in fact."

"Well, that's nice to know, anyway."

She said, "Hey, what's taking so long?"

He said, "Just wait."

"I'm getting dizzy and sleepy."

"Wait."

When he appeared again, he had crossed his eyes and was clutching an imaginary something to his chest. She laughed. "Harpo."

"No."

"Stumbly."

"There's no such thing as Stumbly."

"Okay," she said, laughing, delighting in him. "Who then?"

"How could you say Harpo?"

"I'm sorry."

"Harpo," he said. "Jeez."

"All right, who is it, then?"

"It's my uncle Mark."

"I never met your uncle Mark."

"Never met Stumbly, either."

She laughed again. "You win."

"No," he said. "Who's this?" And he went back into the bathroom.

She waited, a little impatiently now. She was beginning to feel uncomfortable, and she didn't want to get too sleepy. In fact, there was a heavy, buzzing sensation in her ears when she closed her eyes.

"Boo," he said. He had mussed his hair and made it stand on end, and he was wearing his shirt like a cape around his neck. He went through the pantomime motions of lighting a cigarette, and then she saw that he meant her to understand it was dope, not tobacco. He fake-puffed, rolled his eyes, breathed with a thick, throaty rasping, and held his index finger and thumb in the pose of passing a joint. "Well?" he said.

"I'm thinking."

"This is no ordinary cigarette."

"I can't think of his name. The Supreme Court guy."

"Wrong," he said, smoothing his hair down. He went back into the bathroom, but then leaned out, holding on to the frame, and smiled at her. "You know what you get when you cross a doctor with a ground hog?"

"A court date," she said, laughing.

"Somebody told you," he said.

"Is that *it?*"

"Six more weeks of golf," he said.

"I don't get it. Tell me another one."

"You know what you get if you mix rock 'n' roll and Dorsey?" His eyebrows went up. He seemed to be taking great delight in the question. "You get stumbly."

"Howard," she said.

He disappeared into the bathroom again.

"Hey," she called, getting to her feet. This time he leaned out the door, bending low, so that he was looking at her from a horizontal angle. He tipped an imaginary hat and said, "You slept with Dorsey before you got married, huh. That's the stumbly truth, sort of."

"Stop talking about Dorsey," she said. "Stop that."

He grinned at her. "Wouldn't be surprised if you went out and met him while we were engaged. I mean, you know. Talking to him on the phone and stuff. You and old Dorsey maybe decided to play a little for old time's sake. A little stumbly on the side?"

"What?" she said to him. "What?"

He lifted his chin slightly, as if to challenge her.

"Look," she said, "This isn't funny. I know you don't mean it but it's not in the least bit amusing."

He had disappeared past the frame.

"Howard," she said.

Now he let himself fall out of the frame, catching himself at the last possible second with one hand. Again, he tipped an imaginary hat. "Dorsey has beautiful hands, and you made some rock 'n' roll behind my back."

"Howard, stop this."

He was laughing; he had pulled himself up and was out of sight again. She moved toward the bed, so that she could see into where he was. But now he came out, walking unsteadily, carrying his folded shirt and pants.

"Howard," she said.

He turned to her, his face an impassive, confident mask. "Wait," he said.

"Howard, say you're sorry."

"You're sorry," he said.

"I mean it," she told him.

He went to the bed and dropped down on it again, clasped his hands behind his head, and seemed to wait for her to speak. But he spoke first. "Strip."

"What?"

"Go ahead. Strip for me."

She said nothing.

"Come on. Dance—turn me on a little."

"Look," she said.

"Hey—look," he said. "I mean it. I really want you to." His face was bright and innocent-looking and friendly, as if he were a child asking for candy. She had a moment of doubting that she could have heard everything quite exactly.

"Honey," she said. "You're teasing me."

He crossed his legs. "I'm not teasing—come on, this is our honeymoon, right? I've been waiting for this."

"You—" she began.

"Look, what's the situation here," he said.

"You're not like this, Howard, now stop it."

"Well," he said. "Maybe I am teasing."

"Don't tease like that anymore," she told him. "I don't like it."

"Aren't you drunk?" he said. He was lying there staring at her. "Didn't you strip for Dorsey?"

She turned, started fumbling with the door.

"Hey," he said.

She couldn't get the door to work; at some point she'd put the chain on. He got off the bed and came up behind her. She was crying. He wrapped his arms around her, was holding her, kissing the back of her neck. "Let go of me," she said.

"Don't be mad."

"Let go of me, Howard."

He stepped back. She pulled the hair away from her face,

feeling sour now—sodden and dizzy and alone. She was leaning against the door, crying, and he simply stood there with that open-faced boy's expression, staring at her. "Hey," he said. "I was just teasing you."

"Teasing," she said. "Teasing. Right. Jesus Christ."

"I was teasing. Didn't you know I was teasing?"

She looked at him.

"Hey," he said. "Come on." He took hold of her elbow, was leading her back into the room, and she had an eerie, frightful moment of sensing that he considered himself to be in a kind of mastery over her. She resisted, pulled away from him. "Don't touch me."

"Hey," he said not unkindly. "I said I was sorry."

"You said those horrible things—"

He sat down on the bed and locked his hands between his knees. "Let's start over, okay? This is supposed to be a honeymoon night."

She stood there.

"We were having so much fun. Weren't we? Weren't we having fun?"

It was impossible to return his gaze. Impossible to look into those blue boy's eyes.

"I got drunk, okay? I went too far."

"I don't feel good," she said. "I have to go to the bathroom."

"Want me to go for you?"

"No." She was crying, holding it in, moving toward the bathroom door. The light in that little tiled space looked like refuge. He stood and moved in front of her, reaching to hold the door open. "Oh, hey," he said. "I've got one."

She halted, sniffled, felt the closeness of the room.

"Do you have to go really bad?"

"I just want to be alone for a while," she said.

"You don't have to go?"

"Howard, for God's sake."

"Well, no—but look. I've got one more. You've got to see it. It's funny. Stay here."

"I don't want to play anymore," she told him.

"Yeah, but wait'll you see this one."

"Oh, stop it," she said, crying. "Please."

"You'll see," he told her, turning his bright, happy expression away, moving into the bathroom ahead of her and hunching down, working himself up somehow.

"Oh, please," she said, crying, watching him with his back turned there in the bright light of the bathroom.

"Wait, now," he said. "Let me think a minute. I'll have one in a minute." He wavered slightly and brought his hands up to his face. "It'll be funny," he said. "Don't look. I'm thinking."

"Just let's go to sleep," she told him.

"Let me concentrate," he said. "Jesus. I promise you'll like it and laugh."

She waited, feeling a deeper and deeper sense of revulsion. It was the champagne, of course; she'd had so much of it and they were both drunk, and people said and did things when they'd had too much. She was trying to keep this clear in her mind, feeling the sickness start in her and watching him in his bent, agitated posture. He turned slightly and regarded her. "Don't stare," he said. "I can't concentrate if you stare."

"What are you doing?" she asked him. But she had barely spoken; the words had issued forth from her like a breath.

"I had it a minute ago," he said, hunching his shoulders, shifting slightly, running his hands through his hair. Watching this, she had an unpleasant little thought, which arrived almost idly in the boozy haze and irritation of the moment, but which quickly blossomed into a fright more profound than she could have dreamed—and which some part of her struggled with a deep shudder to blot out—that he looked like one of those scarily adept comedians on television, the ones who faced themselves away from the camera and gyrated a moment, then whirled around and were changed, had become the semblance of someone else, spoke in an accent or with a different voice, or had donned a mask or assumed a contorted facial expression, looking like anyone at all but themselves.

OLD WEST

1950

DON'T let my age or my clothes fool you. I've traveled the world. I've read all the books and tried all the counsels of the flesh, too. I've been up and I've been down and I've lived to see the story of my own coming of age in the Old West find its way into the general mind, if you will. In late middle age, for a while, I entertained on the vaudeville stage, telling that story. It's easy to look past an old man now, I know. But in those days I was pretty good. The Old West was my subject. I had that one story I liked to tell, about Shane coming into our troubled mountain valley. You know the story. Well, I was the one, the witness. The little boy. I had come from there, from that big sky, those tremendous spaces, and I had seen it all. And yet the reason I could tell the story well enough to work in vaudeville with it was that I no longer quite believed it.

What I have to tell now is about that curious fact.

I've never revealed any of this before. Back then, I couldn't have, because it might've threatened my livelihood; and later I didn't because—well, just because. But the fact is, he came back to the valley twelve, thirteen years later. Joe Starrett was dead of the cholera, and though Mother and I were still living on the place, there really wasn't much to recommend it anymore. You couldn't get corn or much of anything green to grow. That part of the world was indeed cattle country and for all the bravery of the homesteaders, people had begun to see this at last.

We'd buried Joe Starrett out behind the barn, and Mother didn't want to leave him there, wouldn't move to town. Town, by the way, hadn't really changed, either: the center of it was still Grafton's one all-purpose building—though, because it was the site of the big gunfight, it had somewhat of the aspect of a museum about it now, Grafton having left the bullet hole in the wall and marked out the stains of blood on the dusty floor. But it was still the center of activity, still served as the saloon and general store, and lately, on Sundays, it had even become a place of worship.

I should explain this last, since it figures pretty prominently in what happened that autumn I turned twenty-one: One day late in the previous winter a short, squat old bird who called himself the Right Reverend Bagley rode into the valley on the back of a donkey and within a week's time was a regular sight on Sunday, preaching from the upstairs gallery of the saloon. What happened was, he walked into Grafton's, ordered a whiskey and drank it down, then turned and looked at the place: five or six cowhands, the cattle baron's old henchmen, and a whore that Grafton had brought back with him from the East that summer. (Nobody was really *with* anybody; it was early evening. The sun hadn't dropped below the mountains yet.) Anyway, Bagley turned at the bar and looked everybody over, and then he announced in a friendly but firm tone that he considered himself a man of the gospel, and it was his opinion that this town was in high need of some serious saviorizing. I wasn't there, but I understand that Grafton, from behind the bar, asked him what he meant, and that Bagley began to explain in terms that fairly mesmerized everyone in the place. (It is true that the whore went back East around this time, but nobody had the courage—or the meanness—to ask Grafton whether or not there was a connection.)

But as I was saying, the town wasn't much, and it wasn't going to *be* much. By now everybody had pretty well accepted this. We were going on with our lives, the children were growing up and leaving, and even some of the older ones, the original homesteaders who had stood and risked themselves for all of it alongside Joe Starrett, who had withstood the pressure of the cattlemen, had found reasons to move on. It's simple enough to say why: the winters were long and harsh; the ground, as I said, was stingy; there were better things beyond the valley (we had heard, for instance, that in San Francisco people were riding electric cars to the tops of buildings; Grafton claimed to have seen one in an exhibit in New York).

I was restless. It was just Mother and me in the cabin, and we weren't getting along too well. She'd gone a little crazy with Joe Starrett's death; she wasn't even fifty yet, but she looked at least fifteen years older than that. In the evenings she wanted me with her, and I wanted to be at Grafton's. Most of the men in the valley were spending their evenings there. We did a lot of heavy drinking back in those days. A lot of people stayed drunk most of the time during the week. Nobody felt very good in the mornings. And on Sundays we'd go aching and sick back to Grafton's, the place of our sinful pastimes, to hear old Bagley preach. Mother, too. The smell of that place on a Sunday—the mixture of perfume and sweat and whiskey, and the deep effluvium of the spittoons, was enough to make your breathing stop at the bottom of your throat.

Life was getting harder all the time, and we were not particularly deserving of anything different, and we knew it.

Sometimes the only thing to talk about was the gunfight, though I'm willing to admit that I had contributed to this; I was, after all, the sole witness, and I did discover over the years that I liked to talk about it. It was history, I thought. A story—my story. I could see everything that I remembered with all the clarity of daytime sight, and I *believed* it. The principal actors, through my telling, were fixed forever in the town's lore—if you could call it lore. Three of them were still buried on the hill outside town, including Wilson, the gunfighter who was so fast on the draw and who was shot in the blazing battle at Grafton's by the quiet stranger who had ridden into our valley and changed it forever.

HE came back that autumn, all those years later, and, as before, I was the first to see him coming, sitting atop that old paint of his, though of course it wasn't the same horse. Couldn't have been. Yet it was old. As a matter of harsh fact, it was, I would soon find out, a slightly swaybacked mare with a mild case of lung congestion. I was mending a fence out past the creek, standing there in the warm sun, muttering to myself, thinking about going to town for some whiskey, and I saw him far off, just a slow-moving speck at the foot of the mountains. Exactly like the first time. Except that I was older, and maybe half as curious. I had pretty much taken the attitude of the valley: I was reluctant to face anything new—suspicious of change, afraid of the unpredictable. I looked off at him as he approached and thought of the other time, that first time. I couldn't see who it was, of course, and had no idea it would actually turn out to be him, and for a little aching moment I wanted it to *be* him— but as he was when I was seven; myself as I was then. The whole time back, and Joe Starrett chopping wood within my hearing, a steady man, good and strong, standing astride his own life, ready for anything. I stood there remembering this, some part of me yearning for it, and soon he was close enough to see. I could just make him out. Or rather, I could just make out the pearl-handled six-shooter. Stepping away from the fence, I waited for him, aching, and then quite suddenly I wanted to signal him to turn around, find another valley. I wasn't even curious. I knew, before I could distinguish the changed shape of his body and the thickened features of his face, that he would be far different from my memory of him, and I recalled that he'd left us with the chance for some progress, the hope of concerning ourselves with the arts of peace. I thought of my meager town, the years of idleness in Grafton's store. I wasn't straight or tall, particularly. I was just a dirt farmer with no promise of much and no gentleness or good wishes anymore, plagued with a weakness for whiskey.

Nothing could have prepared me for the sight of him.

The shock of it took my breath away. His buckskins were frayed and torn, besmirched with little maplike continents of salt stains and sweat. He was huge around the middle— his gunbelt had been stretched to a small homemade hole he'd made in it so he could still wear it—and the flesh under his chin was swollen and heavy. His whole face seemed to have dropped and gathered around his jaws, and when he lifted his hat I saw the bald crown of his head through his blowing hair. Oh, he'd gone very badly to seed. "You wouldn't be—" he began.

"It's me all right," I said.

He shifted a little in the saddle. "Well."

"You look like you've come a long way," I said.

He didn't answer. For a moment, we simply stared at each other. Then he climbed laboriously down from the nag and stood there holding the reins.

"Where does the time go," he said, after what seemed a hopeless minute.

Now I didn't answer. I looked at his boots. The toes were worn away; it was all frayed, soiled cloth there. I felt for him. My heart went out to him. And yet as I looked at him I knew that more than anything, more than my oldest childhood dream and ambition, I didn't want him there.

"Is your father—" he hesitated, looked beyond me.

"Buried over yonder," I said.

"And Marian?" He was holding his hat in his hands.

"Look," I said. "What did you come back for, anyway?"
He put the hat back on. "Marian's dead, too?"
"I don't think she'll be glad to see you," I said. "She's settled into a kind of life."
He looked toward the mountains, and a little breeze crossed toward us from the creek. It rippled the water there and made shadows on it, then reached us, moved the hair over his ears. "I'm not here altogether out of love," he said.
I thought I'd heard a trace of irony in his voice. "Love?" I said. "Really?"
"I mean love of the valley," he told me.
I didn't say anything. He took a white handkerchief out of his shirt—it was surprisingly clean—and wiped the back of his neck with it, then folded it and put it back.
"Can I stay here for a few days?" he asked.
"Look," I said. "It's complicated."
"You don't want me to stay even a little while?"
I said nothing for a time. We were just looking at each other across the short distance between us. "You can come up to the cabin," I told him. "But I need some time to prepare my mother for this. I don't want—and you don't want—to just be riding in on her."
"I understand," he said.

MOTHER had some time ago taken to sitting in the window of the cabin with my old breech-loading rifle across her lap. When she'd done baking the bread and tending the garden, when she'd finished milking the two cows and churning the butter, when the eggs were put up and the cabin was swept and clean and the clothes were all hanging on the line in the yard, she'd place herself by the window, gun cocked and ready to shoot. Maybe two years earlier, some poor, lost, starved, lone Comanche had wandered down from the north and stopped his horse at the edge of the creek, looking at us, his hands visored over his eyes. He was easily ninety years old, and when he turned to make his way west along the creek, on out of sight, Mother took my rifle off the wall, loaded it, and set herself up by the window.

"Marian," I said. "It was just an old brave looking for a good place to die."

"You let me worry about it, son."

Well, for a while that worked out all right, in fact; it kept her off me and my liquid pursuits down at Grafton's. She could sit there and take potshots at squirrels in the brush all day if she wanted to, I thought. But in the last few months it had begun to feel dangerous approaching the cabin at certain hours of the day and night. You had to remember that she was there, and sometimes, coming home from Grafton's, I'd had enough firewater to forget. I had her testimony that I had nearly got my head blown off more than once, and once she had indeed fired upon me.

This had happened about a week before he came back into the valley, and I felt it then as a kind of evil premonition—I should say I *believe* I felt it that way, since I have the decades of hindsight now, and I do admit that the holocaust which was coming to us might provide anyone who survived it with a sense that all sorts of omens and portents preceded the event. In any case, the night Marian fired on me, I was ambling sleepily along, drunk, barely able to hold on to the pommel, and letting the horse take me home. We crossed the creek and headed up the path to the house. The shot nicked me above the elbow—a tiny cut of flesh that the bullet took out as it went singing off into the blackness behind me. The explosion, the stinging crease of the bullet just missing bone, and the shriek of my horse sent me flying into the water of the creek.

"I got you, you damn savage Indian," Marian yelled from the cabin.

I lay there in the cold water and reflected that my mother

had grown odd. "Hey!" I called, staying low, hearing her put another shell into the breech. "It's me! It's your son!"

"I got a repeating rifle here," she lied. She'd reloaded and was aiming again. I could actually hear it in her voice. "I don't have any children on the place."

There is no sound as awful and startling as the sound of a bullet screaming off rock, when you know it is aimed earnestly at you.

"Wait!" I yelled. "Goddammit, Marian, it's me! For God's sake, it's your own family!"

"Who?"

"Your son," I said. "And you've wounded me."

"I don't care what he's done," she said and fired again. The bullet buzzed overhead like a terribly purposeful insect.

"Remember how you didn't want any more guns in the valley?" I shouted. "You remember that, Mother? Remember how much you hate them?"

She said, "Who is that down there?"

"It's me," I said. "Good Christ, I'm shot."

She fired again. This one hit the water behind me and went off skipping like a piece of slate somebody threw harder than a thing can be thrown. "Blaspheming marauders!" she yelled.

"It's me!" I screamed. "I'm sick. I'm coming from Grafton's. I'm shot in the arm."

I heard her reload, and then there was a long silence.

"Marian?" I said, keeping low. "Would you shoot your own son dead?"

"How do I know it's you?"

"Well, who else would it be at this hour?"

"You stay where you are until I come down and see, or I'll blow your head off," she said.

So I stayed right where I was, in the cold running creek, until she got up the nerve to approach me with her lantern and her cocked rifle. Only then did she give in and tend to me, her only son, nearly killed, hurting with a wound she herself had inflicted.

"You've been to Grafton's drinking that whiskey," she said, putting the lantern down.

"You hate guns," I told her. "Right?"

"I'm not letting you sleep it off in the morning, either."

"Just don't shoot at me," I said.

But she had already started up on something else. That was the way her mind had gone over the years, and you never knew quite how to take her.

AND so that day when he rode up, I told him to stay out of sight and went carefully back up to the cabin. "Mother," I said. "Here I come."

"In here," she said from the barn. She was churning butter, and she simply waited for me to get to the window and peer over the sill. I did so, the same way I almost always did now: carefully, like a man in the middle of a gunfight.

"What?" she said. "What?"

I had decided during my stealthy course up the path that my way of preparing her for his return would be to put her out of the way of it, if I could. Any way I could. She was sitting there in the middle of the straw-strewn floor with a floppy straw hat on her head as though the sun were beating down on her. Her hands looked so old, gripping the butter churn. "Mother," I said. "The Reverend Bagley wants you to bring him some bread for Sunday's communion."

"Who's dead?"

On top of everything else, of course, she'd begun to lose her hearing. I repeated myself, fairly shrieking it at her.

"Bagley always wants that," she said, looking away. "I take the bread over on Saturdays. This isn't Saturday. You don't need to yell."

"It's a special request," I said. "He needs it early this

week." If I could get her away from the cabin now, I could make some arrangements. I could find someplace else for our return visitor to stay. I could find out what he wanted, and then act on it in some way. But I wasn't really thinking very clearly. Marian and old Bagley had been seeing each other for occasional Saturday and Sunday afternoon picnics, and some evenings, too. There could have been no communication between Bagley and me without Marian knowing about it. I stood there trying to think up some other pretext, confused by the necessity of explaining the ridiculous excuse for a pretext I had just used, and she came slowly to her feet, sighing, touching her back low, shaking her head, turning away from me.

"Hitch the team up," she said.

It took a moment for me to realize that she'd actually believed me. "I can't go with you," I told her.

"You don't expect me to go by myself." She wiped her hands on the front of her dress. "Go on. Hitch the team."

"All right," I said. I knew there would be no arguing with her. She'd set herself to my lie, and once her mind was set you couldn't alter or change it. Besides, I was leery of giving her too much time to ponder over things. I'd decided the best thing was to go along and deal with everything as it came. There was a chance I could get away after we got to town; I could hightail it back home and make some adjustment or some arrangement. "I have to tie off what I'm doing with the fence," I told her. "You change, and I'll be ready."

"You're going to change?"

"You change."

"You want *me* to change?"

"You've got dirt all over the front of you."

She shook her head, lifted the dress a little to keep it out of the dust, and made her slow way across to the cabin. When she was inside, I tore over to the fence and found him sitting his horse, nodding, half dozing, his hat hanging from the pommel of his saddle, his sparse hair standing up in the wind. He looked a little pathetic.

"Hey," I said, a little louder than I had to, I admit.

He tried to draw his pistol. The horse jumped, stepped back, coughing. His hand missed the pearl handle, and then the horse was turning in a tight circle, stomping his hat where it had fallen, and he sat there holding on to the pommel, saying, "Whoa. Hold it. Damn. Whoa, will you?" When he got the horse calmed, I bent down and retrieved his hat.

"Here," I said. "Lord."

He slapped the hat against his thigh, sending off a small white puff of dust, then put it on. The horse turned again, so that now his back was to me.

"For God's sake," I said. "Why don't you get down off him?"

"Damn spooky old paint," he said, getting it turned. "Listen, boy, I've come a long way on him. I've slept on him and just let him wander where he wanted. I've been that hungry and that desperate." The paint seemed to want to put him down as he spoke. I thought it might even begin to buck.

"Look," I said. "We need to talk. We don't have a lot of time, either."

"I was hoping I could ride up to the cabin," he said.

I shook my head. "Out of the question."

"No?"

"Not a chance," I said.

He got down. The paint coughed like an old sick man, stepped away from us, put its gray muzzle down in the saw grass by the edge of the water, and began to eat.

"A little congestion," he said.

The paint coughed into the grass.

"I can't ride in?"

"On that?"

He looked down.

"Look," I said. "It would upset her. You might get your head shot off."

He stared at me. "Marian has a gun?"

"Marian shoots before she asks questions these days," I said.

"What happened?" he wanted to know.

"She got suspicious," I said. "How do I know?" And I couldn't keep the irritation out of my voice.

He said nothing.

"You can use the barn," I told him. "But you have to wait until we leave, and you can't let her see you. You're just going to have to take my word for it."

Again he took the hat off, looking down. Seeing the freckles on his scalp, I wished he'd put it back on.

"Wait here and keep out of sight until you see us heading off toward town," I said. I couldn't resist adding, "There's a preacher who likes her, and she likes him back." I watched his face, remembering with a kind of sad satisfaction the way—as I had so often told it—he'd leaned down to me, bleeding, from his horse and said, "Tell your mother there's no more guns in the valley."

He put the hat back on.

I said, "I'm hoping she'll be tied up with him for a while, anyway, until I can figure something out."

"Who's the preacher?" he said, staring.

"There's nothing you can do about it," I said.

"I'd just like to know his name."

I said the name, and he nodded, repeating it almost to himself. "Bagley."

"Now will you do as I say?" I asked.

"I will," he said. "If you'll do something for me." And now I saw a little of the old fire in his eyes. It sent a thrill through me. This was, after all, the same man I remembered single-handedly killing the old cattle baron and his hired

gunfighter in the space of a half second. I had often talked
about the fact that while my shouted warning might have
been what saved him from the backshooter aiming at him
from the gallery, the shot he made—turning into the explosion and smoke of the ambush and firing from reflex, almost
as if the Colt in his flashing hand had simply gone off by
accident—was the most astonishing feat of gun handling and
shooting that anyone ever saw: one shot, straight through
the backshooter's heart, and the man toppled from that gallery like a big sack of feed, dead before he even let go of his
still smoking rifle. That was how I had told the story; that
was how I remembered everything.

"All right," I said.

He took a step away from me, then removed his hat again,
stood there smoothing its brim, folding it, or trying to. "This
Bagley," he said over his shoulder. "How long's he been
here?"

"I don't know," I said, and I didn't exactly. Nobody ever
counted much time in those days, beyond looking for the
end of winter, the cold that kills. "Sometime last winter, I
guess."

"He's your preacher."

"I guess."

"Ordained?"

In those days, I didn't know the word.

"What church is he with?"

"No church," I said. "Grafton's. His own church."

"Set up for himself, then."

"Every Sunday. He preaches from the gallery."

"Does he wear a holster?"

"Not that I know of."

"You ever see him shoot?"

"No," I said. Then: "Listen, shooting the preacher won't
change anything."

He gave me a look of such forlorn unhappiness that I almost corrected myself. "Maybe I won't be staying very long at all," he said.

"Just wait here," I told him.

He nodded, but he wasn't looking at me.

On the way to town, I kept thinking of the hangdog way he'd stood watching me go back to the cabin for Marian—the vanquished look of his face and the dejection in his bowed stance. I wasn't prepared to think I could've so defeated him with news, or with words. Certainly there was something else weighing him down. Marian rode along beside me, staring off at the mountains, her rough, red hands lying on her lap. To tell the truth, I didn't want to know what she might be thinking. Those days, if asked, she was likely to begin a tirade. There was always something working on her sense of well-being and symmetry. Entropy and decline were everywhere. She saw evil in every possible guise. Moral decay. Spiritual deprivation and chaos. Along with her window sitting, armed to the teeth and waiting for marauders, I'm afraid she'd started building up some rather strange hostilities toward the facts of existence: there had even been times, over the years, when I could have said she meant to demand all the rights and privileges of manhood, and I might not have been far from wrong. That may sound advanced, to your ears; in her day, it was cracked. In any case, way out there in the harsh, hard life of the valley, I had managed to keep these more bizarre aspects of her decline from general knowledge. And I'd watched with gladness her developing attachment to old Bagley, who had a way of agreeing with her without ever committing himself to any of it.

"So," she said now. "Why'd you want to get me away from the house?"

For a moment I couldn't speak.

"I can't believe you remember it's the anniversary of our coming here."

Now I was really dumbfounded. Things had worked into my hands, in a way, and I was too stupefied to take advantage of the fact.

"Well?" she said.

I stammered something about being found out in my effort to surprise her, then went on to make up a lie about taking her to Grafton's for a glass of the new bottled Coke soda. Grafton had tried some of it on his last trip to New York and had been stocking it ever since. Now and then Marian liked to be spoiled, driven in the wagon to some planned destination and treated like a lady. For all her crazy talk, she could be sweet sometimes; she could remember how things were when Joe Starrett was around and she was his good wife.

"We're not going to see Bagley?"

"We can stop by and see him," I said.

The team pulled us along the road. It was a sunny day, clear and a little chilly. She turned and looked behind us in that way she had sometimes of sensing things. "Look," she said.

It was the dust of a lone rider, a long way off, following, gaining on us. I didn't allow myself to think anything about it.

"I thought I heard you talking to somebody down at the spring," she said. "Could this be him?"

"Who?" I said. It was amazing how often her difficulty hearing yielded up feats of overhearing, long distances bridged by some mysterious transmutation of her bad nerves and her suspicions.

"I don't know," she said. "Whoever you were talking to."

"I wasn't talking to anybody," I said, and I knew I sounded guilty.

"I thought I heard something," she mumbled, turning again to look behind us.

I had ahold of the reins, and without having to think about

it I started flapping them a little against the hindquarters of the team. We sped up some.

"What're you doing?" she said. "It's not Indians, is it?"

We were going at a pretty good gait now.

"It's Comanches," she said, breathless, reaching into her shawl and bringing out a big six-shot Colt. It was so heavy for her that she had to heft it with both hands.

"Where in God's name did you get that thing?" I said.

"Bagley gave it to me for just this purpose."

"It's not Indians," I said. "Jesus. All the Indians are peaceful now anyway."

She was looking back, trying to get the pistol aimed that way and managing only to aim it at me.

"Will you," I said, ducking. "Marian."

"Just let me get turned," she said.

When she had got it pointed behind us, she pulled the hammer back with both thumbs. It fired, and it was so unwieldy in her hands, going off toward the blue sky as she went awry on the seat, that it looked like something that had got ahold of her.

"Marian!" I yelled.

The team was taking off with us; it was all I could do to hold them. She was getting herself right in the seat again, trying to point the Colt.

"Give me that," I said.

"Faster!" she screamed, firing again. This time she knocked part of a pine branch off at the rim of the sky. Under the best circumstances, if she'd been aiming for it and had had the time to draw a good bead on it, anyone would have said it was a brilliant shot. But it knocked her back again, and I got hold of the hot barrel of the damn thing and wrenched it from her.

"All right!" she yelled. "Goddammit, give me the reins, then!"

I suppose she'd had the time to notice, during her attempts

to kill him on the run, that he was quickly catching up to us. Now he came alongside me, and he had his own Colt drawn. I dropped Marian's into the well of the wagon seat and pulled the team to a halt, somehow managing to keep Marian in her place at my side. She was looking at him now, but I don't think she recognized him. Her face was registering relief—I guess at the fact that he wasn't a Comanche.

He still had his gun drawn. "So," he said. "You were going to warn him."

"What the hell are you talking about?" I said. I was pretty mad now. "Will you put that Colt away, please?"

He kept it where it was, leveled at me.

"I know," I said. "I'm going to get shot. It must be God's plan. First her, and now you."

"You were shooting at me."

"No, he wasn't," Marian said. "I was."

He looked at her, then smiled. It was a sad, tentative, disappointed smile. I don't think he could quite believe what time had done to her. She was staring back at him with those fierce, cold, pioneer-stubborn, unrecognizing eyes. "Marian?" he said.

"What."

"You were going to warn him, weren't you."

"Warn who?" I said.

"She knows." He looked past me at her. "Well, Marian?"

"I can't believe it," she said. "After all these years. Look at you. What happened to you?"

He said nothing to this.

"Will you please holster your Colt," I said to him.

"Marian," he said, doing as I asked with the Colt. "You were going to tell him I was here, right?"

"Will somebody tell me what's going on here?" I said.

Marian stared straight ahead, her hands folded on her lap. "My son was taking me to Grafton's for a bottle of Coke soda."

"That's the truth," I said to him. "I was trying to spare her the shock of seeing you. I told you I had to make some arrangements."

"I—I was sorry to hear about Joe," he said, looking past me again.

"Joe," she said. She merely repeated the name.

He waited.

"She thought you were an Indian," I said.

"I'm here to get a man named Phegley—self-styled preacher. Squarish, small build. Clean-shaven. Rattlery voice. I was hired to chase him, and I think I chased him here."

"This one's name is Bagley," I said. "And he's got a beard."

"He's used other names. Maybe he's grown a beard. I'll know him on sight."

Through all this Marian simply stared at him, her hands still knotted on her lap. "You're going to kill him," she said now.

"I'm going to take him back to Utah, if he'll come peacefully."

"Look at you," she said. "I just don't believe it."

"You haven't changed at all," he said. It was almost charming.

"I don't believe it," my mother said under her breath.

He got down off his horse and tied it to the back of the wagon, then climbed up on the back bench.

"I hope you don't mind," he said, nodding politely.

"We really are going to Grafton's," I said.

"That's fine."

"I don't think Bagley will be there."

"I'm sure I'll run into him sooner or later."

"If somebody doesn't warn the poor man," Marian said.

"Well," he said. "Phegley—or Bagley—will use a pistol."

Then we were just going along toward town. In a way, we were as we had once been—or we were a shade of it.

The wagon, raising its long column of dust, and the horse trotting along, tethered to the back. I held the reins as Joe Starrett had held them, and wondered what the woman seated to my right could be thinking about.

BAGLEY lived in a little shed out in back of the stables. The smell of horses was on him all the time, though he never did any riding to speak of, and he never quite got himself clean enough for me to be able to stand him at close quarters for very long. Back then, of course, people could go several seasons without feeling it necessary to be anywhere near the vicinity of a bath, and Bagley was one of them. On top of this, he was argumentative and usually pretty grumpy and ill-tempered. And for some reason—some unknown reason fathomable only to her, and maybe, to give him the credit of some self-esteem, to Bagley, too—Marian liked him. He had a way of talking to her as if the two of them were in some sort of connivance about things (I had heard him do this, had marveled at it, wondered about it). And he'd done some reading. He'd been out in the world, and around some. He'd told Marian that when he was a younger man, he'd traveled to the farthest reaches of the north and got three of his toes frozen off, one on one foot and two on the other. Marian said she'd seen the proof of this. I didn't care to know more.

What I found interesting was the fact that Bagley was usually available for our late-night rounds of whiskey drinking and was often enough among the red-eyed and half-sick the following morning—even, sometimes, Sunday morning. In fact, it was when he was hung over that he could be really frightening as an evangelist; the pains of hell, which he was always promising for all sinners, were visible in his face: "Hold on, brethren, for this here is the end times!" he'd shout. "This is the last of civilized humankind. Hold on.

We've already broken the chain! The end has already begun. Hold on. Storms are coming! War! New ways of killing! Bombs that cause the sun to blot out, hold on! I said, Hold on! Death falling from the sky and floating up out of the ground! I don't believe you heard me, brethren. Plagues and wars and bunched towns clenched on empty pleasures and fear, it's on its way, just hold on! Miseries and diseases we ain't even named! Pornography and vulgar worship of possessions, belief in the self above everything else, abortion, religious fraud, fanatic violence, mass murder, and killing boredom, it's all coming, hold on! Spiritual destitution and unbelievable banality, do hold on!"

He was something.

And you got the feeling he believed it all: when he really got going, he looked like one of those crazed, half-starved prophets come back from forty days and nights in the desert.

I hadn't had a lot to do with him in the time he'd been in town, but I had told him the story of the gunfight. It was on one of those nights we were all up drinking whiskey and talking. We were sitting in Grafton's around the stove, passing a bottle back and forth. It was late. Just Grafton and Bagley and me. I went through the whole story: the cattle baron and his badmen trying to run us all off, and the stranger riding into the valley and siding with us, the man with the pearl-handled Colt and the quick nervous hands who seemed always on the lookout for something. The arrival of Wilson, a killer with the cold blood of a poisonous snake. And the inevitable gunfight itself, my memory of Wilson in black pants with a black vest and white shirt, drawing his Colt, and the speed of the hands that beat him to the draw. Bagley listened, staring at me like consternation itself.

"Wilson was fast," I said to him. "Fast on the draw."

"Young man, you should tell stories of inspiration and good works. Do I detect a bit of exaggeration in your story?"

"Exaggeration," I said. I couldn't believe I was being challenged.

"A little stretching of things, maybe?"

"Like what?" I said, angry now.

"I don't know. What about this Wilson? Was he really so cold-blooded?"

"He shot a man dead outside on the street. He picked a fight with him and then slaughtered him with no more regard than you'd give a bug. We buried the poor man the day before the fight."

"And this Wilson—he wore black?"

I nodded. "Except for the white shirt."

"I knew a Wilson," he said. "Of course, that's a common name. But this one was a sort of professional gunfighter, too. Sort of. Not at all like the one you describe. I heard he was shot somewhere out in the territories, a few years back."

This had the effect of making me quite reasonlessly angry, as though Bagley were trying to cast some doubt on me. It also troubled something in my mind, which glimmered for a second and then went on its unsettling way. I was drunk. There were things I didn't want to talk about anymore. I was abruptly very depressed and unhappy.

"What is it, son?" he said.

"Nothing."

He leaned back in his chair and drank from the bottle we had all been passing around.

"I seem to remember Wilson as wearing buckskins," Grafton said.

"No," I said. "He was wearing black pants and a black vest over a white shirt. And he had a two-gun rig."

"Well," said Bagley. "The Wilson I knew carried this old heavy Colt. Carried it in his pants."

"Come to think of it, I don't believe I remember two guns on him," said Grafton.

"It was two guns," I said. "I saw them. I was there."

"Boy *was* there," Grafton said to Bagley. "You have to hand him that."

"Must not be the same Wilson," Bagley said.

"You ever been in a gunfight, Reverend?" Grafton asked him.

"No, I usually run at the first sign of trouble."

"Do you own a gun?" I asked him.

He shook his head. "I had one once. Matter of fact, this Wilson fellow—the one I knew—he gave it to me. Come to think of it, he had three of them. And he carried them all on his person. But the one he used most was always stuck down in his belt."

"Why would he give you a Colt?" I asked him.

"I don't recall. Seems to me I won it from him, playing draw poker. We were both a little drunk. He could be an amiable old boy, too. Give you the shirt off his back if he was in a good mood. Trouble was, he wasn't often disposed to be in a good mood."

"Was he fast on the draw?" I asked.

He made a sound in his throat, cleared it, looking at me. "You read a lot, do you?"

"Some," I lied. I was barely able to write my name, then, for all Marian's early efforts.

"Well," said Bagley, clearing his throat again. "I seem to recall that when old Wilson was upset he was quick to shoot people, if that's what you mean."

"Was he fast?"

"I don't think he thought in those terms. He usually had his six-shooter out and already cocked if he thought there would be any reason to use it."

Grafton said, "You know quite a bit about this sort of thing, don't you, Reverend?"

Bagley nodded, folding his pudgy hands across his chest.

He looked at me. "I guess I saw some things over the years of my enslavement to the angels of appetite and sin."

"But you were never in a gunfight?"

"I said I usually run."

"Did you ever find yourself in a circumstance where you couldn't run?"

"Once or twice," he said, reaching for the bottle.

"And?" I said.

He smiled, drank, wiped his whiskered mouth. "Why, I shot from ambush, of course." Then he laughed loud, offering me the bottle. "There are several states of this tragic and beautiful union which I am not particularly anxious to see again."

"Do you mean you're wanted?" Grafton asked him.

"I don't really know," he said. "It's been a long time. And I've traveled so far."

WHEN he wasn't preaching, he seemed fairly inactive. Marian had never had any trouble figuring where he'd be. His sole support was what he could collect on Sunday, and what he could make helping out with the work of keeping the stables. He was fond of saying that no task was too low for sinners. Sometimes when he preached, if he wasn't getting on about the dire troubles the world was heading for, he was inclined to talk about the dignity provided by simple work. He could be almost sweet about that sort of idea. And sometimes, too, he talked about odd, unconnected things: Galileo and Napoleon; the new English queen; the tragic early death of the English writer, Dickens. Everything was a lesson. He'd fix you with his old, hooded eyes, and his thin lips would begin to move, as though he were chewing something unpalatable that was hurting his gums, and then he would begin to talk, the sentences lining up one after the other, perfectly symmetrical and organized as well as any written speech. We had all got to trusting him, not as the figure we could look to for succor or solace, particularly, but as a predictable and consistent form of diversion, of entertainment.

At least that was how I felt about him.

And so some coloration of that feeling was rising in me as I drove the wagon into town and stopped in front of Grafton's, wondering if Bagley was there and what would happen if indeed he was. The street was empty. There weren't even any other horses around. Wind picked up dust and carried it in a drunken spiral across the way, where the dirt lane turned toward the stables.

"Grafton," Marian called, getting down. "You open or not?"

The door was ajar. She went up on the wooden sidewalk and down to the end of it, looked up and down that part of the crossing street. She waited there a minute. Then she came back and went into the saloon. In the wagon now it was just me and our returning visitor.

I said, "Tell me. What did Bagley—Phegley—do?"

"I can't say I know for sure. His name was posted. There's a reward."

"How much?" I asked.

He shrugged. "Six hundred dollars dead."

"And alive?"

"Five hundred twenty-five."

I looked at him.

"It was a private post."

"And you don't even know what he did?"

"I could use the extra seventy-five dollars," he said. "But I'm willing to take him back alive."

"You're—you're a peace officer, then?"

He shook his head, looking beyond me at the tall facade of Grafton's building.

"Is it personal?" I said.

"It's business," he mumbled. "Old business, too."

"Listen," I said. "Where'd you go when you left us that day? After the fight here."

He looked at me. "Fight?"

I waited.

He seemed to consider a moment. "Chinook Falls, I guess."

"Chinook Falls?" I said. "That's the next town over. That's only a day's ride."

He nodded. "Guess it is."

"How long did you stay there?"

Again, he thought a moment. "I don't know—four or five years, maybe."

"Four or five years?"

"I got married."

I stared at him.

"Yep. Got married and settled down awhile. But she wasn't much for sitting around in the evenings."

"She left you."

"In a way," he said. "I guess so."

"What happened?"

"Got sick on gin," he muttered, chewing on something he'd brought out of his shirt pocket; it looked like a small piece of straw. "Got real sick on gin one night. Died before I could do much of anything for her."

A moment later I said, *"Then* where'd you go?"

He shrugged, took the piece of straw from his mouth. "Around."

"Around where?" I asked, and he named several other towns, not one of which was farther than two days' ride from where we were sitting.

"That's it?" I said.

He nodded, not quite looking at me. "Pretty much."

"You're just a bounty hunter," I said. "Right?"

And he gave me a quizzical look, as if he hadn't understood the question. "What do you think?"

"Well, for God's sake," I said. "And you wanted me to grow straight and tall."

"You were a little boy. That's what you say to little boys. Some of them do, you know. Some of them grow straight and tall. Look at Joe Starrett."

"I don't want to think about that," I said. "I was thinking about you."

Now Marian came out of the saloon, and behind her Grafton stood, looking worried. "Don't come in," he said. "I don't want any trouble here. I'm too old for it." He squinted, peering at us.

"We're looking for Bagley," I said. By now I simply wanted to see what would happen.

"I don't think you should come here."

"Is he in there?" I said.

"He's where he always is this time of day," Grafton said. "The stables, sleeping it off."

Marian had climbed back onto the wagon seat. "Took me a strain getting that much out of him," she muttered. Then she turned to me. "Take me to the stables."

"Wait," said Grafton. "I'm coming along, too." And he hurried down and climbed up into the back of the wagon, arranging his besmirched white apron over his knees.

So it was the four of us who rode around to the stables and pulled up at the shady, open entrance. We sat there for a while. Then Marian got down and stood in the rising dust and looked at me. "I'm going to go tell him we're here."

"He's a man who will use a gun," Shane said.

"This isn't your man," said Marian.

And Bagley's voice came from one of the windows above the street, I couldn't see which one. "Who wants to see the preacher?"

Now Grafton got down, too. He and Marian were standing there next to the wagon.

"Bagley," I said. "There's a man here looking for somebody named—"

But then Marian went running toward the open doorway. "Don't shoot!" she yelled. "Don't anybody shoot!"

Grafton had moved to take hold of her arms as she swept past him. She was dragging him with her toward the shade of the building.

From the nearest window, I saw Bagley's black gun barrel jutting out.

"Everybody just be calm!" Marian was shouting. "Let's all just wait a little bit! Please!"

But nobody waited for anything. Bagley fired from the window and the bullet hit the planks just below my foot. I have no idea what he could've been trying to hit, but I assumed he had through some mistake been aiming at me, so I dove into the back of the wagon—and there I collided painfully with the balding, deeply lined face of my childhood hero.

I had struck him on the bridge of the nose with my forehead, and instantly there was blood. It covered both of us. We looked at each other. I saw blind, dumb terror in his eyes. All around us was the roar of gunfire, explosions that seemed to come nearer, and we were crouching there, bloody and staring at each other. "Save me," I said, feeling all the more frightened for what I saw in his eyes—the scared little life there, wincing back from danger, sinking, showing pain and confusion and weakness, too. I never hated any face more, all my long life.

I had been a boy when the other thing happened. I had remembered it a certain way all those years, and had told the story a certain way, and now, here, under the random explosive, struck-wood sound of ricocheting bullets, I was

being given something truer than what I'd held in my mind
all that time.

At least that is what I've been able to make of it. I know
that everything seemed terribly familiar, and that something
about it was almost derisively itself, as if I could never have
experienced it in any fashion but like this, face down in a
wagon bed with my hands over my head.

"Everybody shut up!" Marian was yelling. "Everybody
stop!"

From somewhere came the sound of someone reloading,
and I heard Bagley's voice. "One, two, three." His voice was
imbued with an eerie kind of music, like happiness.

"Bagley!" I screamed. "It's me!"

"I'm going to have to shoot all of you," he said. "That's
the way it's going to have to be now. Unless you turn that
wagon around and get out fast. And take him with you."

"John Bagley, you listen to me," Marian said from somewhere in the dust.

But then everything was obliterated in the din, the tumult
which followed. It seemed to go on and on, and to grow
louder. I didn't know where anyone was. I lay there in the
wagon bed and cried for my life, and then it was over and
in the quiet that followed—the quiet that was like something
muffled on the eardrums, a physical feeling, a woolly, prickly
itch on the skin, coupled with the paralyzed sense of a dread-
ful dumbfoundedness—I heard my own murmuring, and
came to understand that I had survived. After a long wait,
I stood in the wagon bed and looked at Marian sitting, alive
and untouched, in the dust of the street, her hands held tight
over her ears like a child trying to drown out the thunderous
upheaval of a storm. Poor Grafton was sitting against one of
the bales of hay by the stable door, his hands open on his
thighs as though he had just paused there to get out of the
brilliant autumn sun that was beating down out of the quiet
sky. Bagley lay in the upstairs window, his head lolling down

over the pocked sill. A stray breeze stirred his hair. The man who had brought his gun back into the valley lay at the back wheel of the wagon, face up to the light, looking almost serene. The whole thing had taken ten seconds, if that.

I HAVE come from there to here.

I helped Marian up onto the wagon seat and drove her home. We didn't say anything; we didn't even go near each other for several days (and then it was only to stare across the table at each other while we ate the roast she'd made; it was as if we were both afraid of what might be uncovered if we allowed ourselves to speak at all). Someone else, I don't know—someone from the town—took the others away and buried them. The next time I went into town, Grafton's was closed, and people were sitting around on the sidewalk in front, leaning against the side of the building. Apparently Grafton's whore was challenging the arrangements or something: nobody could touch a thing in the place until it got settled, one way or the other. Anyway, it wasn't going to be Grafton's anymore.

Some years later, when she'd grown too tired and too confused to know much of anything, Marian passed on quietly in her sleep. I buried her with Joe Starrett out behind the barn of that place. I traveled far away from the valley— much farther than the next town—and never went back. I have grown old. My life draws back behind me like a long train. I never knew what it was Shane intended for himself, nor what Bagley had done to be posted, nor what had caused him to open fire that way, any more than I was ever to know what poor Grafton must've thought when he dropped down in the street with the bullet in his lungs.

When I think of it, though, I find a small truth that means more to me than all my subsequent reading, all my late studies to puzzle out the nature of things: of course, nothing could be simpler, and perhaps it is already quite obvious to you, but what I remember now, in great age, is that during the loudest and most terrifying part of the exchange of shots, when the catastrophe was going on all around me and I was most certain that I was going to be killed, I lay shivering in the knowledge, the discovery really, that the story I'd been telling all my life was in fact not true enough—was little more than a boy's exaggeration.

And this is what I have come to tell you.

That the clearest memory of my life is a thing I made up in my head. For that afternoon at the stables, in the middle of terror, with the guns going off, I saw it all once again, without words, the story I'd been telling and that I'd believed since I was seven years old, only this time it was just as it had actually been. I saw again the moment when the gunfighter Wilson went for his Colt, and he was indeed not all in black, not wearing two guns nor any holster, but sloppily draped in some flannels of such faded color as to be not quite identifiable. I saw it like a searing vision, what it had *really* been—a man trying to get a long-barreled pistol out of the soiled tangle of his pants, catching the hammer of it on the tail of his shirt. And the other, the hero, struggling with his own weapon, raising it, taking aim, and firing—that shattering detonation, a blade of fire from the end of the pistol, and Wilson's body crashing down between a chair and table. The hero then turning to see the cattle baron on the other side of the room reach into his own tight coat, and a boy watching the hero raise his heavy Colt to fire upon the cattle baron, too—the cattle baron never even getting his weapon clear of the shoulder holster he had.

And it was all over. Like murder, nothing more.

Do you see? No backshooter firing from the gallery. Just the awful moment when the cattle baron realized he would be shot. And the boy who watched from under the saloon door saw the surprised, helpless, frightened look on the old whiskered face, saw this and closed his eyes, hearing the second shot, the second blast, squeezing his eyes shut for fear of looking upon death anymore, but hearing the awful, clattering fall and the stillness that followed, knowing what it was, what it meant, and hearing, too, now, the little other sounds—the settling in of ragged breath, the sigh of relief. Beginning, even then, in spite of himself—in spite of what he had just seen—to make it over in his young mind, remembering it already like all the tales of the Old West, the story as he would tell it for more than eighty years, even as he could hear the shaken voice, almost garrulous, of the one who had managed to stay alive—the one who was Shane, and who, this time, hadn't been killed in the stupid, fumbling blur of gunfighting.

DESIGN

THE Reverend Tarmigian was not well. You could see it in his face—a certain hollowness, a certain blueness in the skin. His eyes lacked luster and brightness. He had a persistent dry, deep cough; he'd lost a lot of weight. And yet on this fine, breezy October day he was out on the big lawn in front of his church, raking leaves. Father Russell watched him from the window of his study, and knew that if he didn't walk over there and say something to him about it, this morning— like so many recent mornings—would be spent fretting and worrying about Tarmigian, seventy-two years old and out raking leaves in the windy sun. He had been planning to speak to the old man for weeks, but what could you say to a man like that? An institution in Point Royal, old Tarmigian had been pastor of the neighboring church—Faith Baptist, only a hundred or so yards away on the other side of Tallawaw Creek—for more than three decades. He referred to himself in conversation as the Reverend Fixture. He was a stooped, frail man with wrinkled blue eyes and fleecy blond hair that showed freckled scalp in the light; there were dimples in his cheeks. One of his favorite jokes—one of the many jokes he was fond of repeating—was that he had the eyes of a clown built above the natural curve of a baby's bottom. He'd touch the dimples and smile, saying a thing like that. And the truth was he tended to joke too much—even about the fact that he was apparently taxing himself beyond the dictates of good health for a man his age.

It seemed clear to Father Russell—who was all too often

worried about his own health, though he was thirty years younger than Tarmigian—that something was driving the older man to these stunts of killing work: raking leaves all morning in the fall breezes; climbing on a ladder to clear drainspouts; or, as he had done one day last week, lugging a bag of mulch across the road and up the hill to the little cemetery where his wife lay buried, as if there weren't plenty of people within arm's reach on any Sunday who would have done it gladly for him (and would have just as gladly stood by while he said his few quiet prayers over the grave). His wife had been dead twenty years, he had the reverential respect of the whole countryside, but something was driving the man and, withal, there was often a species of amused cheerfulness about him almost like elation, as though he were keeping some wonderful secret.

It was perplexing; it violated all the rules of respect for one's own best interest. And today, watching him rake leaves, Father Russell determined that he would speak to him about it. He would simply confront him—broach the subject of health and express an opinion. Father Russell understood enough about himself to know that this concern would seem uncharacteristically personal on his part—it might even be misconstrued in some way—but as he put a jacket on and started out of his own church, it was with a small thrill of resolution. It was time to interfere, regardless of the age difference and regardless of the fact that it had been Father Russell's wish to find ways of avoiding the company of the older man.

Tarmigian's church was at the top of a long incline, across a stone bridge over Tallawaw Creek. It was a rigorous walk, even on a cool day, as this one was. The air was blue and cool in the mottled shade, and there were little patches of steam on the creek when the breezes were still. The Reverend Tarmigian stopped working, leaned on the handle of the rake and watched Father Russell cross the bridge.

"Well, just in time for coffee."

"I'll have tea," Father Russell said, a little out of breath from the walk.

"You're winded," said Tarmigian.

"And you're white as a sheet."

It was true. Poor Tarmigian's cheeks were pale as death. There were two blotches on them, like bruises—caused, Father Russell was sure, by the blood vessels that were straining to break in the old man's head. He indicated the trees all around, burnished-looking and still loaded with leaves, and even now dropping some of them, like part of an argument for the hopelessness of this task the old man had set for himself.

"Why don't you at least wait until they're finished?" Father Russell demanded.

"I admit, it's like emptying the ocean with a spoon." Tarmigian put his rake down and motioned for the other man to follow him. They went through the back door into the older man's tidy little kitchen, where Father Russell watched him fuss and worry, preparing the tea. When it was ready, the two men went into the study to sit among the books and talk. It was the old man's custom to take an hour every day in this book-lined room, though with this bad cold he'd contracted, he hadn't been up to much of anything recently. It was hard to maintain his old fond habits, he said. He felt too tired, or too sick. It was just an end-of-summer cold, of course, and Tarmigian dismissed it with a wave of his hand. Yet Father Russell had observed the weight loss, the coughing; and the old man was willing to admit that lately his appetite had suffered.

"I can't keep anything down," he said. "Sort of keeps me discouraged from trying, you know? So I shed the pounds. I'm sure when I get over this flu—"

"Medical science is advancing," said the priest, trying for sarcasm. "They have doctors now with their own offices and instruments. It's all advanced to a sophisticated stage. You can even get medicine for the flu."

"I'm fine. There's no need for anyone to worry."

Father Russell had seen denial before: indeed, he saw some version of it almost every day, and he had a rich understanding of the psychology of it. Yet Tarmigian's statement caused a surprising little clot of anger to form in the back of his mind and left him feeling vaguely disoriented, as if the older man's blithe neglect of himself were a kind of personal affront.

Yet he found, too, that he couldn't come right out and say what he had come to believe: that the old man was jeopardizing his own health. The words wouldn't form on his lips. So he drank his tea and searched for an opening—a way of getting something across about learning to relax a bit, learning to take it easy. There wasn't a lot to talk about beyond Tarmigian's anecdotes and chatter. The two men were not particularly close: Father Russell had come to his own parish from Boston only a year ago, believing this small Virginia township to be the accidental equivalent of a demotion (the assignment, coming really like the drawing of a ticket out of a hat, was less than satisfactory). He had felt almost immediately that the overfriendly, elderly clergyman next door was a bit too southern for his taste—though Tarmigian was obviously a man of broad experience, having served in missions overseas as a young man, and it was true that he possessed a kind of simple, happy grace. So while the priest had spent a lot of time in the first days trying to avoid him for fear of hurting his feelings, he had learned finally that Tarmigian was unavoidable, and had come to accept him as one of the mild irritations of the place in which he now found himself. He had even considered that the man had a kind of charm, was amusing and generous. He would admit that there had been times when he found himself surprised by a faint stir of gladness when the old man could be seen on the little crossing bridge, heading down to pay another of his casual visits as if there were nothing better to do than to sit in Father Russell's parlor and make jokes about himself.

The trouble now, of course, was that everything about the old man, including his jokes, seemed tinged with the something terrible that the priest feared was happening to him. And here Father Russell was, watching him cough, watching him hold up one hand as if to ward off anything in the way of advice or concern about it. The cough took him deep, so that he had to gasp to get his breath back; but then he cleared his throat, sipped more of the tea and, looking almost frightfully white around the eyes, smiled and said, "I have a good one for you, Reverend Russell. I had a couple in my congregation—I won't name them, of course—who came to me yesterday afternoon, claiming they were going to seek a divorce. You know how long they've been married? They've been married fifty-two years. Fifty-two years and they say they can't stand each other. I mean can't stand to be in the same room with each other."

Father Russell was interested in spite of himself—and in spite of the fact that the old man had again called him "Reverend." This would be another of Tarmigian's stories, or another of his jokes. The priest felt the need to head him off. "That cough," he said.

Tarmigian looked at him as if he'd merely said a number or recited a day's date.

"I think you should see a doctor about it."

"It's just a cold, Reverend."

"I don't mean to meddle," said the priest.

"Yes, well. I was asking what you thought about a married couple can't stand to be in the same room together after fifty-two years."

Father Russell said, "I guess I'd have to say I have trouble believing that."

"Well, believe it. And you know what I said to them? I said we'd talk about it for a while. Counseling, you know."

Father Russell said nothing.

"Of course," said Tarmigian, "as you know, we permit divorce. Something about an English king wanting one badly enough to start his own church. Oh, that was long ago, of course. But we do allow it when it seems called for."

"Yes," Father Russell said, feeling beaten.

"You know, I don't think it's a question of either one of them being interested in anybody else. There doesn't seem to be any romance or anything—nobody's swept anybody off anybody's feet."

The priest waited for him to go on.

"I can't help feeling it's a bit silly." Tarmigian smiled, sipped the tea, then put the cup down and leaned back, clasping his hands behind his head. "Fifty-two years of marriage, and they want to untie the knot. What do you say, shall I send them over to you?"

The priest couldn't keep the sullen tone out of his voice. "I wouldn't know what to say to them."

"Well—you'd tell them to love one another. You'd tell them that love is the very breath of living or some such thing. Just as I did."

Father Russell muttered, "That's what I'd have to tell them, of course."

Tarmigian smiled again. "We concur."

"What was their answer?"

"They were going to think about it. Give themselves some time to think, really. That's no joke, either." Tarmigian laughed, coughing. Then it was just coughing.

"That's a terrible cough," said the priest, feeling futile and afraid and deeply irritable. His own words sounded to him like something learned by rote.

"You know what I think I'll tell them if they come back?"

He waited.

"I think I'll tell them to stick it out anyway, with each other." Tarmigian looked at him and smiled. "Have you ever heard anything more absurd?"

Father Russell made a gesture, a wave of the hand, that he hoped the other took for agreement.

Tarmigian went on: "It's probably exactly right—probably exactly what they should do, and yet such odd advice to think of giving two people who've been together fifty-two years. I mean, when do you think the phrase 'sticking it out' would stop being applicable?"

Father Russell shrugged and Tarmigian smiled, seemed to be awaiting some reaction.

"Very amusing," said Father Russell.

But the older man was coughing again.

From the beginning there had been things Tarmigian said and did which unnerved the priest. Father Russell was a man who could be undone by certain kinds of boisterousness, and there were matters of casual discourse he simply would never understand. Yet often enough over the several months of their association, he had entertained the suspicion that Tarmigian was harboring a bitterness, and that his occasional mockery of himself was some sort of reaction to it, if it wasn't in fact a way of releasing it.

Now Father Russell sipped his tea and looked away out the window. Leaves were flying in the wind. The road was in blue shade, and the shade moved. There were houses beyond the hill, but from here everything looked like a wilderness.

"Well," Tarmigian said, gaining control of himself. "Do you know what my poor old couple say is their major complaint? Their major complaint is they don't like the same TV programs. Now, can you imagine a thing like that?"

"Look," the priest blurted out. "I see you from my study window—you're—you don't get enough rest. I think you should see a doctor about that cough."

Tarmigian waved this away. "I'm fit as a fiddle, as they say. Really."

"If it's just a cold, you know," said Father Russell, giving up. "Of course—" he could think of nothing else to say.

"You worry too much," Tarmigian said. "You know, you've got bags under your eyes."

TRUE.

In the long nights Father Russell lay with a rosary tangled in his fingers and tried to pray, tried to stop his mind from playing tricks on him: the matter of greatest faith was and had been for a very long time now that every twist or turn of his body held a symptom, every change signified the onset of disease. It was all waiting to happen to him, and the anticipation of it sapped him, made him weak and sick at heart. He had begun to see that his own old propensity for morbid anxiety about his health was worsening, and the daylight hours required all his courage. Frequently he thought of Tarmigian as though the old man were in some strange way a reflection of his secretly held, worst fear. He recalled the lovely sunny mornings of his first summer as a curate, when he was twenty-seven and fresh and the future was made of slow time. This was not a healthy kind of thinking. It was middle age, he knew. It was a kind of spiritual dryness he had been taught to recognize and contend with. Yet each morning his dazed wakening—from whatever fitful sleep the night had yielded him—was greeted with the pall of knowing that the aging pastor of the next-door church would be out in the open, performing some strenuous task as if he were in the bloom of health. When the younger man looked out the window, the mere sight of the other building was enough to make him sick with anxiety.

*   *   *

ON Friday Father Russell went to Saint Celia Hospital to attend to the needs of one of his older parishioners, who had broken her hip in a fall, and while he was there a nurse walked in and asked that he administer the sacrament of extreme unction to a man in the emergency room. He followed her down the hall and the stairs to the first floor, and while they walked she told him the man had suffered a heart attack, that he was already beyond help. She said this almost matter-of-factly, and Father Russell looked at the delicate curve of her ears, thinking about design. This was, of course, an odd thing to be contemplating at such a somber time, yet he cultivated the thought, strove to concentrate on it, gazing at the intricacy of the nurse's red-veined ear lobe. Early in his priesthood, he had taught himself to make his mind settle on other things during moments requiring him to look upon sickness and death—he had worked to foster a healthy appreciation of, and attention to, insignificant things which were out of the province of questions of eternity and salvation and the common doom. It was what he had always managed as a protection against too clear a memory of certain daily horrors—images that could blow through him in the night like the very winds of fright and despair—and if over the years it had mostly worked, it had recently been in the process of failing him. Entering the crowded emergency room, he was concentrating on the whorls of a young woman's ear as an instrument for hearing, when he saw Tarmigian sitting in one of the chairs near the television, his hand wrapped in a bandage, his pallid face sunk over the pages of a magazine.

Tarmigian looked up, then smiled, held up the bandaged hand. There wasn't time for the two men to speak. Father Russell nodded at him and went on, following the nurse, feeling strangely precarious and weak. He looked back over his shoulder at Tarmigian, who had simply gone back to reading the magazine, and then he was attending to what the nurse had brought him to see: she pulled a curtain aside to reveal a gurney with two people on it—a man and a woman of roughly the same late middle age—the woman cradling the man's head in her arms and whispering something to him.

"Mrs. Simpson," the nurse said, "here's the priest."

Father Russell stood there while the woman regarded him. She was perhaps fifty-five, with iron gray hair and small, round, wet eyes. "Mrs. Simpson," he said to her.

"He's my husband," she murmured, rising, letting the man's head down carefully. His eyes were open wide, as was his mouth. "My Jack. Oh, Jack. Jack."

Father Russell stepped forward and touched her shoulder, and she cried, staring down at her husband's face.

"He's gone," she said. "We were talking, you know. We were thinking about going down to see the kids. And he just put his head down. We were talking about how the kids never come to visit and we were going to surprise them."

"Mrs. Simpson," the nurse said, "would you like a sedative? Something to settle your nerves—"

This had the effect of convincing the poor woman about what had just taken place: the reality of it sank into her features as the color drained from them. "No," she said in a barely audible whisper, "I'm fine."

Father Russell began quickly to say the words of the sacrament, and she stood by him, gazing down at the dead man.

"I—I don't know where he is," she said. "He just put his head down." Her hands trembled over the cloth of her husband's shirt, which was open wide at the chest, and it was a moment before Father Russell understood that she was trying to button the shirt. But her hands were shaking too much. She patted the shirt down, then bowed her head and sobbed. Somewhere in the jangled apparatus of the room something was beeping, and he heard air rushing through pipes; everything was obscured in the intricacies of procedure. And then he was simply staring at the dead man's blank countenance, all sound and confusion and movement falling away from him. It was as though he had never looked at anything like this before; he remained quite still, in a profound quiet, for some minutes before Mrs. Simpson got his attention again. She had taken him by the wrist.

"Father," she was saying. "Father, he was a good man. God has taken him home, hasn't He?"

Father Russell turned to face the woman, to take her hands into his own and to whisper the words of hope.

"I THINK seeing you there—at the hospital," he said to Tarmigian. "It upset me in an odd way."

"I cut my hand opening the paint jar," Tarmigian said. He was standing on a stepladder in the upstairs hallway of his rectory, painting the crown molding. Father Russell had walked out of his church in the chill of first frost and made his way across the little stone bridge and up the incline to the old man's door, had knocked and been told to enter, and, entering, finding no one, had reached back and knocked again.

"Up here," came Tarmigian's voice.

And the priest had climbed the stairs in a kind of torpor, his heart beating in his neck and face. He had blurted out that he wasn't feeling right, hadn't slept at all well, and finally he'd begun to hint at what he could divine as to why. He was now sitting on the top step, hat in hand, still carrying with him the sense of the long night he had spent, lying awake in the dark, seeing not the dead face of poor Mrs. Simpson's husband but Tarmigian holding up the bandaged hand and smiling. The image had wakened him each time he had drifted toward sleep.

"Something's happening to me," he said now, unable to believe himself.

The other man reached high with the paint brush, concentrating. The ladder was rickety.

"Do you want me to hold the ladder?"

"Pardon me?"

"Nothing."

"Did you want to know if I wanted you to hold the ladder?"

"Well, do you?"

"You're worried I'll fall."

"I'd like to help."

"And did you say something is happening to you?"

Father Russell was silent.

"Forget the ladder, son."

"I don't understand myself lately," said the priest.

"Are you making me your confessor or something there, Reverend?"

"I—I can't—"

"Because I don't think I'm equipped."

"I've looked at the dead before," said Father Russell. "I've held the dying in my arms. I've never been very much afraid of it. I mean I've never been morbid."

"Morbidity is an indulgence."

"Yes, I know."

"Simply refuse to indulge yourself."

"I'm forty-three—"

"A difficult age, of course. You don't know whether you fit with the grown-ups or the children." Tarmigian paused to cough. He held the top step of the ladder with both hands, and his shoulders shook. Everything tottered. Then he stopped, breathed, wiped his mouth with the back of one hand.

Father Russell said, "I meant to say, I don't think I'm worried about myself."

"Well, that's good."

"I'm going to call and make you an appointment with a doctor."

"I'm fine. I've got a cold. I've coughed like this all my life."

"Nevertheless."

Tarmigian smiled at him. "You're a good man—but you're learning a tendency."

No peace.

Father Russell had entered the priesthood without the sort of fervent sense of vocation he believed others had. In fact, he'd entertained serious doubts about it right up to the last year of seminary—doubts that, in spite of his confessor's reassurances to the contrary, he felt were more than the normal upsets of seminary life. In the first place, he had come to it against the wishes of his father, who had entertained dreams of a career in law for him; and while his mother applauded the decision, her own dream of grandchildren was visibly languishing in her eyes as the time for his final vows approached. Both parents had died within a month of each other during his last year of studies, and so there had been times when he'd had to contend with the added problem of an apprehension that he might unconsciously be learning to use his vocation as a form of refuge. But finally, nearing the end of his training, seeing the completion of the journey, something in him rejoiced, and he came to believe that this was what having a true vocation was: no extremes of emotion, no real perception of a break with the world, though the terms of his faith and the ancient ceremony that his training had prepared him to celebrate spoke of just that. He was even-tempered and confident, and when he was ordained, he set about the business of being a parish priest. There were matters to involve himself in, and he found that he could be energetic and enthusiastic about most of them. The life was satisfying in ways he hadn't expected, and if in his less confident moments some part of him entertained the suspicion that he was not progesssing spiritually, he was also not the sort of man to go very deeply into such questions: there were things to do. He was not a contemplative. Or he hadn't been.

Something was shifting in his soul.

Nights were terrible. He couldn't even pray now. He stood at his rectory window and looked at the light in the old man's window, and his imagination presented him with the belief that he could hear the faint rattle of the deep cough, though he knew it was impossible across that distance. When he said the morning mass, he leaned down over the host and had to work to remember the words. The stolid, calm faces of his parishioners were almost ugly in their absurd confidence in him, their smiles of happy expectation and welcome. He took their hospitality and their care of him as his due, and felt waves of despair at the ease of it, the habitual taste and lure of it, while all the time his body was aching in ways that filled him with dread and reminded him of Tarmigian's ravaged features.

Sunday morning early, it began to rain. Someone called, then hung up before he could answer. He had been asleep; the loud ring at that hour had frightened him, changed his heartbeat. He took his own pulse, then stood at his window and gazed at the darkened shape of Tarmigian's church. That morning after the second mass, exhausted, miserable, filled with apprehension, he crossed the bridge in the rain, made his way up the hill and knocked on the old man's door. There wasn't any answer. He peered through the window on the porch and saw that there were dishes on the table in the kitchen, which was visible through the arched hallway off the living room. Tarmigian's Bible lay open on the arm of the easy chair. Father Russell knocked loudly and then walked around the building, into the church itself. It was quiet. The wind stirred outside and sounded like traffic whooshing by. Father Russell could feel his own heartbeat in the pit of his stomach. He sat down in the last pew of

Tarmigian's church and tried to calm himself. Perhaps ten minutes went by, and then he heard voices. The old man was coming up the walk outside, talking to someone. Father Russell stood, thought absurdly of trying to hide, but then the door was opened and Tarmigian walked in, accompanied by an old woman in a white woolen shawl. Tarmigian had a big umbrella, which he shook down and folded, breathing heavily from the walk and looking, as always, even in the pall of his decline, amused by something. He hadn't seen Father Russell yet, though the old woman had. She nodded and smiled broadly, her hands folded neatly over a small black purse.

"Well," Tarmigian said. "To what do we owe this honor, Reverend?"

It struck Father Russell that they might be laughing at him. He dismissed this thought and, clearing his throat, said, "I—I wanted to see you." His own voice sounded stiffly formal and somehow foolish to him. He cleared his throat again.

"This is Father Russell," Tarmigian said loudly to the old woman. Then he touched her shoulder and looked at the priest. "Mrs. Aldenberry."

"God bless you," Mrs. Aldenberry said.

"Mrs. Aldenberry wants a divorce," Tarmigian murmured.

"Eh?" she said. Then, turning to Father Russell, "I'm hard of hearing."

"She wants her own television set," Tarmigian whispered.

"Pardon me?"

"And her own room."

"I'm hard of hearing," she said cheerfully to the priest. "I'm deaf as a post."

"Irritates her husband," Tarmigian said.

"I'm sorry," said the woman, "I can't hear a thing."

Tarmigian guided her to the last row of seats, and she sat

down there, folded her hands in her lap. She seemed quite content, quite trustful, and the old minister, beginning to stutter into a deep cough, winked at Father Russell—as if to say this was all very entertaining. "Now," he said, taking the priest by the elbow, "Let's get to the flattering part of all this—you walking over here getting yourself all wet because you're worried about me."

"I just wanted to stop by," Father Russell said. He was almost pleading. The old man's face, in the dim light, looked appallingly bony and pale.

"Look at you," said Tarmigian. "You're shaking."

Father Russell could not speak.

"Are you all right?"

The priest was assailed by the feeling that the older man found him somehow ridiculous—and he remembered the initial sense he'd had, when Tarmigian and Mrs. Aldenberry had entered, that he was being laughed at. "I just wanted to see how you were doing," he said.

"I'm a little under the weather," Tarmigian said, smiling.

And it dawned on Father Russell, with the force of a physical blow, that the old man knew quite well he was dying.

Tarmigian indicated Mrs. Aldenberry with a nod of his head. "Now I have to attend to the depths of this lady's sorrow. You know, she says she should've listened to her mother and not married Mr. Aldenberry fifty-two years ago. She's revising her own history; she can't remember being happy in all that time, not now, not after what's happened. Now you think about that a bit. Imagine her standing in a room slapping her forehead and saying 'What a mistake!' Fifty-two years. Oops. A mistake. She's glad she woke up in time. Think of it! And I'll tell you, Reverend, I think she feels lucky."

Mrs. Aldenberry made a prim, throat-clearing sound, then stirred in her seat, looking at them.

"Well," Tarmigian said, straightening, wiping the smile from his face. He offered his hand to the priest. "Shake hands. No. Let's embrace. Let's give this poor woman an ecumenical thrill."

Father Russell shook hands, then walked into the old man's extended arms. It felt like a kind of collapse. He was breathing the odor of bay rum and talcum and something else, too, something indefinable and dark, and to his astonishment he found himself fighting back tears. The two men stood there while Mrs. Aldenberry watched, and Father Russell was unable to control the sputtering and trembling that took hold of him. When Tarmigian broke the embrace, the priest turned away, trying to compose himself. Tarmigian was coughing again.

"Excuse me," said Mrs. Aldenberry. She seemed quite tentative and upset.

Tarmigian held up one hand, still coughing, and his eyes had grown wide with the effort to breathe.

"Hot honey with a touch of lemon and whiskey," she said, to no one in particular. "Works like a charm."

Father Russell thought about how someone her age would indeed learn to feel that humble folk remedies were effective in stopping illness. It was logical and reasonable, and he was surprised by the force of his own resentment of her for it. He stood there wiping his eyes and felt his heart constrict with bitterness.

"Well," Tarmigian said, getting his breath back.

"Hot toddy," said Mrs. Aldenberry. "Never knew it to fail." She was looking from one to the other of the two men, her expression taking on something of the look of tolerance. "Fix you up like new," she said, turning her attention to the priest, who could not stop blubbering. "What's—what's going on here?"

Father Russell had a moment of sensing that everything Tarmigian had done or said over the past year was somehow freighted with this one moment, and it took him a few seconds to recognize the implausibility of such a thing: no one could have planned it, or anticipated it, this one seemingly aimless gesture of humor—out of a habit of humorous gestures, and from a brave old man sick to death—that could feel so much like health, like the breath of new life.

He couldn't stop crying. He brought out a handkerchief and covered his face with it, then wiped his forehead. It had grown quiet. The other two were gazing at him. He straightened, caught his breath. "Excuse me."

"No excuse needed," Tarmigian said, looking down. His smile seemed vaguely uncertain now, and sad. Even a little afraid.

"What is going on here?" the old woman wanted to know.

"Why, nothing at all out of the ordinary," Tarmigian said, shifting the small weight of his skeletal body, clearing his throat, managing to speak very loudly, very gently, so as to reassure her, but making certain, too, that she could hear him.

THE
FIREMAN'S
WIFE

JANE'S husband, Martin, works for the fire department. He's on four days, off three; on three, off four. It's the kind of shift work that allows plenty of time for sustained recreation, and during the off times Martin likes to do a lot of socializing with his two shift mates, Wally Harmon and Teddy Lynch. The three of them are like brothers: they bicker and squabble and compete in a friendly way about everything, including their common hobby, which is the making and flying of model airplanes. Martin is fanatical about it—spends way too much money on the two planes he owns, which are on the worktable in the garage, and which seem to require as much maintenance as the real article. Among the arguments between Jane and her husband—about money, lack of time alone together, and housework—there have been some about the model planes, but Jane can't say or do much without sounding like a poor sport: Wally's wife, Milly, loves watching the boys, as she calls them, fly their planes, and Teddy Lynch's ex-wife, before they were divorced, had loved the model planes too. In a way, Jane is the outsider here: Milly Harmon has known Martin most of his life, and Teddy Lynch was once point guard to Martin's power forward on their high school basketball team. Jane is relatively new, having come to Illinois from Virginia only two years ago, when Martin brought her back with him from his reserve training there.

This evening, a hot September twilight, they're sitting on lawn chairs in the dim light of the coals in Martin's portable

grill, talking about games. Martin and Teddy want to play
Risk, though they're already arguing about the rules. Teddy
says that a European version of the game contains a wrinkle
that makes it more interesting, and Martin is arguing that
the game itself was derived from some French game.

"Well, go get it," Teddy says, "and I'll show you. I'll bet
it's in the instructions."

"Don't get that out now," Jane says to Martin.

"It's too long," Wally Harmon says.

"What if we play cards," Martin says.

"Martin doesn't want to lose his bet," Teddy says.

"We don't have any bets, Teddy."

"Okay, so let's bet."

"Let's play cards," Martin says. "Wally's right. Risk takes
too long."

"I feel like conquering the world," Teddy says.

"Oh, Teddy," Milly Harmon says. "Please shut up."

She's expecting. She sits with her legs out, holding her
belly as though it were unattached, separate from her. The
child will be her first, and she's excited and happy; she glows,
as if she knows everyone's admiring her.

Jane thinks Milly is spreading it on a little thick at times:
lately all she wants to talk about is her body and what it's
doing.

"I had a dream last night," Milly says now. "I dreamed
that I was pregnant. Big as a house. And I woke up and I
was. What I want to know is, was that a nightmare?"

"How did you feel in the dream?" Teddy asks her.

"I said. Big as a house."

"Right, but was it bad or good?"

"How would you feel if you were big as a house?"

"Well, that would depend on what the situation was."

"The situation is, you're big as a house."

"Yeah, but what if somebody was chasing me? I'd want
to be big, right?"

"Oh, Teddy, please shut up."

"I had a dream," Wally says. "A bad dream. I dreamed I died. I mean, you know, I was dead—and what was weird was that I was also the one who had to call Milly to tell her about it."

"Oh, God," Milly says. "Don't talk about this."

"It was weird. I got killed out at sea or something. Drowned, I guess. I remember I was standing on the deck of this ship talking to somebody about how it went down. And then I was calling Milly to tell her. And the thing is, I talked like a stranger would—you know, 'I'm sorry to inform you that your husband went down at sea.' It was weird."

"How did you feel when you woke up?" Martin says.

"I was scared. I didn't know who I was for a couple of seconds."

"Look," Milly says, "I don't want to talk about dreams."

"Let's talk about good dreams," Jane says. "I had a good dream. I was fishing with my father out at a creek—some creek that felt like a real place. Like if I ever really did go fishing with my father, this is where we would have fished when I was small."

"What?" Martin says after a pause, and everyone laughs.

"Well," Jane says, feeling the blood rise in her face and neck, "I never—my father died when I was just a baby."

"I dreamed I got shot once," Teddy says. "Guy shot me with a forty-five automatic as I was running downstairs. I fell and hit bottom, too. I could feel the cold concrete on the side of my face before I woke up."

Milly Harmon sits forward a little and says to Wally, "Honey, why did you have to tell about having a dream like that? Now *I'm* going to dream about it, I just know it."

"I think we all ought to call it a night," Jane says. "You guys have to get up at six o'clock in the morning."

"What're you talking about?" Martin says. "We're going to play cards, aren't we?"

"I thought we were going to play Risk," Teddy says.

"All right," Martin says, getting out of his chair. "Risk it is."

Milly groans, and Jane gets up and follows Martin into the house. "Honey," she says. "Not Risk. Come on. We'd need four hours at least."

He says over his shoulder, "So then we need four hours."

"Martin, I'm tired."

He's leaning up into the hall closet, where the games are stacked. He brings the Risk game down and turns, holding it in both hands like a tray. "Look, where do you get off, telling everybody to go home the way you did?"

She stands there staring at him.

"These people are our friends, Jane."

"I just said I thought we ought to call it a night."

"Well *don't* say—all right? It's embarrassing."

He goes around her and back out to the patio. The screen door slaps twice in the jamb. She waits a moment and then moves through the house to the bedroom. She brushes her hair, thinks about getting out of her clothes. Martin's uniforms are lying across the foot of the bed. She picks them up, walks into the living room with them and drapes them over the back of the easy chair.

"Jane," Martin calls from the patio. "Are you playing or not?"

"Come on, Jane," Milly says. "Don't leave me alone out here."

"What color armies do you want?" Martin asks.

She goes to the patio door and looks out at them. Martin has lighted the tiki lamps; everyone's sitting at the picnic table in the moving firelight. "Come on," Martin says, barely concealing his irritation. She can hear it, and she wants to react to it—wants to let him know that she is hurt. But they're all waiting for her, so she steps out and takes her place at the table. She chooses green for her armies, and she plays the game to lose, attacking in all directions until her forces are so badly depleted that when Wally begins to make his own move she's the first to lose all her armies. This takes more than an hour. When she's out of the game, she sits for a while, cheering Teddy on against Martin, who is clearly going to win; finally she excuses herself and goes back into the house. The glow from the tiki lamps makes weird patterns on the kitchen wall. She pours herself a glass of water and drinks it down; then she pours more and swallows some aspirin. Teddy sees this as he comes in for more beer, and he grasps her by the elbow and asks if she wants something a little better than aspirin for a headache.

"Like what?" she says, smiling at him. She's decided a smile is what one offers under such circumstances; one laughs things off, pretends not to notice the glazed look in the other person's eyes.

Teddy is staring at her, not quite smiling. Finally he puts his hands on her shoulders and says, "What's the matter, lady?"

"Nothing," she says. "I have a headache. I took some aspirin."

"I've got some stuff," he says. "It makes America beautiful. Want some?"

She says, "Teddy."

"No problem," he says. He holds both hands up and backs away from her. Then he turns and is gone. She hears him begin to tease Martin about the French rules of the game. Martin is winning. He wants Wally Harmon to keep playing, and Wally wants to quit. Milly and Teddy are talking about flying the model airplanes. They know about an air show in Danville on Saturday. They all keep playing and talking, and for a long time Jane watches them from the screen door. She smokes half a pack of cigarettes, and she paces a little. She drinks three glasses of orange juice, and finally she walks into the bedroom and lies down with her face in her hands. Her forehead feels hot. She's thinking about the next four

days, when Martin will be gone and she can have the house
to herself. She hasn't been married even two years, and she
feels crowded; she's depressed and tired every day. She never
has enough time to herself. And yet when she's alone, she
feels weak and afraid. Now she hears someone in the hallway
and she sits up, smoothes her hair back from her face. Milly
Harmon comes in with her hands cradling her belly.

"Ah," Milly says. "A bed." She sits down next to Jane
and then leans back on her hands. "I'm beat," she says.

"I have a headache," Jane says.

Milly nods. Her expression seems to indicate how unim-
portant she finds this, as if Jane had told her she'd already
got over a cold or something. "They're in the garage now,"
she says.

"Who?"

"Teddy, Wally, Martin. Martin conquered the world."

"What're they doing?" Jane asks. "It's almost midnight."

"Everybody's going to be miserable in the morning," Milly
says.

Jane is quiet.

"Oh," Milly says, looking down at herself. "He kicked.
Want to feel it?"

She takes Jane's hand and puts it on her belly. Jane feels
movement under her fingers, something very slight, like one
heartbeat.

"Wow," she says. She pulls her hand away.

"Listen," Milly says. "I know we can all be overbearing
sometimes. Martin doesn't realize some of his responsibilities
yet. Wally was the same way."

"I just have this headache," Jane says. She doesn't want
to talk about it, doesn't want to get into it. Even when she
talks to her mother on the phone and her mother asks how
things are, she says it's all fine. She has nothing she wants
to confide.

"You feel trapped, don't you," Milly says.

Jane looks at her.

"Don't you?"

"No."

"Okay—you just have a headache."

"I do," Jane says.

Milly sits forward a little, folds her hands over the roundness of her belly. "This baby's jumping all over the place."

Jane is silent.

"Do you believe my husband and that awful dream? I wish he hadn't told us about it—now I know I'm going to dream something like it. You know pregnant women and dreams. I begin to shake just thinking of it."

"Try not to think of it," Jane says.

Milly waits a moment and then clears her throat and says, "You know, for a while there after Wally and I were married, I thought maybe I'd made a mistake. I remember realizing that I didn't like the way he laughed. I mean, let's face it, Wally laughs like a hyena. And somehow that took on all kinds of importance—you know, I had to absolutely like everything about him or I couldn't like anything. Have you ever noticed the way he laughs?"

Jane has never really thought about it. But she says nothing now. She simply nods.

"But you know," Milly goes on, "all I had to do was wait. Just—you know, wait for love to come around and surprise me again."

"Milly, I have a headache. I mean, what do you think is wrong, anyway?"

"Okay," Milly says, rising.

Then Jane wonders whether the other woman has been put up to this conversation. "Hey," she says, "did Martin say something to you?"

"What would Martin say?"

"I don't know. I mean, I really don't know, Milly. Jesus Christ, can't a person have a simple headache?"

"Okay," Milly says. "Okay."

"I like the way everyone talks around me here, you know it?"

"Nobody's talking around you—"

"I think it's wonderful how close you all are."

"All right," Milly says, standing there with her hands folded under the bulge of her belly. "You just look so unhappy these days."

"Look," Jane says, "I have a headache, all right? I'm going to go to bed. I mean, the only way I can get rid of it is to lie down in the dark and be very quiet—okay?"

"Sure, honey," Milly says.

"So—goodnight, then."

"Right," Milly says. "Goodnight." She steps toward Jane and kisses her on the cheek. "I'll tell Martin to call it a night. I know Wally'll be miserable tomorrow."

"It's because they can take turns sleeping on shift," Jane says.

"I'll tell them," Milly says, going down the hall.

Jane steps out of her jeans, pulls her blouse over her head and crawls under the sheets, which are cool and fresh and crisp. She turns the light off and closes her eyes. She can't believe how bad it is. She hears them all saying goodnight, and she hears Martin shutting the doors and turning off the lights. In the dark she waits for him to get to her. She's very still, lying on her back with her hands at her sides. He goes into the bathroom at the end of the hall. She hears him cough, clear his throat. He's cleaning his teeth. Then he comes to the entrance of the bedroom and stands in the light of the hall.

"I know you're awake," he says.

She doesn't answer.

"Jane," he says.

She says, "What?"

"Are you mad at me?"

"No."

"Then what's wrong?"

"I have a headache."

"You always have a headache."

"I'm not going to argue now, Martin. So you can say what you want."

He moves toward her, is standing by the bed. He's looming above her in the dark. "Teddy had some dope."

She says, "I know. He offered me some."

"I'm flying," Martin says.

She says nothing.

"Let's make love."

"Martin," she says. Her heart is beating fast. He moves a little, staggers taking off his shirt. He's so big and quick and powerful; nothing fazes him. When he's like this, the feeling she has is that he might do anything. "Martin," she says.

"All right," he says. "I won't. Okay? You don't have to worry your little self about it."

"Look," she says.

But he's already headed into the hall.

"Martin," she says.

He's in the living room. He turns the television on loud. A rerun of *Kojak*. She hears Theo calling someone sweetheart. "Sweetheart," Martin says. When she goes to him, she finds that he's opened a beer and is sitting on the couch with his legs out. The beer is balanced on his stomach.

"Martin," she says. "You have to start your shift in less than five hours."

He holds the beer up. "Baby," he says.

IN the morning he's sheepish, obviously in pain. He sits at the kitchen table with his hands up to his head while she makes coffee and hard-boiled eggs. She has to go to work, too, at a car dealership in town. All day she sits behind a window with a circular hole in the glass, where people line up to pay for whatever the dealer sells or provides, including mechanical work, parts, license plates, used cars, rental cars and, of course, new cars. Her day is long and exhausting, and she's already feeling as though she worked all night. The booth she has to sit in is right off the service bay area, and the smell of exhaust and grease is everywhere. Everything seems coated with a film of grime. She's standing at her sink, looking at the sun coming up past the trees beyond her street, and without thinking about it she puts the water on and washes her hands. The idea of the car dealership is like something clinging to her skin.

"Jesus," Martin says. He can't eat much.

She's drying her hands on a paper towel.

"Listen," he says, "I'm sorry, okay?"

"Sorry?" she says.

"Don't press it, all right? You know what I mean."

"Okay," she says, and when he gets up and comes over to put his arms around her, she feels his difference from her. She kisses him. They stand there.

"Four days," he says.

When Teddy and Wally pull up in Wally's new pickup, she stands in the kitchen door and waves at them. Martin walks down the driveway, carrying his tote bag of uniforms and books to read. He turns around and blows her a kiss. This morning is like so many other mornings. They drive off. She goes back into the bedroom and makes the bed, and puts his dirty uniforms in the wash. She showers and chooses something to wear. It's quiet. She puts the radio on and then decides she'd rather have the silence. After she's dressed, she stands at the back door and looks out at the street. Children are walking to school in little groups of friends. She thinks about the four days ahead. What she needs is to get into the routine and stop thinking so much. She knows that problems in a marriage are worked out over time.

Before she leaves for work she goes out into the garage to look for signs of Teddy's dope. She doesn't want someone stumbling on incriminating evidence. On the worktable along the back wall are Martin's model planes. She walks over and stands staring at them. She stands very still, as if waiting for something to move.

AT work her friend Eveline smokes one cigarette after another, apologizing for each one. During Martin's shifts Jane spends a lot of time with Eveline, who is twenty-nine and single and wants very much to be married. The problem is she can't find anyone. Last year, when Jane was first working at the dealership, she got Eveline a date with Teddy Lynch. Teddy took Eveline to Lum's for hot dogs and beer, and they had fun at first. But then Eveline got drunk and passed out—put her head down on her arms and went to sleep like a child asked to take a nap in school. Teddy put her in a cab for home and then called Martin to laugh about the whole thing. Eveline was so humiliated by the experience that she goes out of her way to avoid Teddy—doesn't want anything to do with him or with any of Martin's friends, or with Martin, for that matter. She will come over to the house only when she knows Martin is away at work. And when Martin calls the dealership and she answers the phone, she's very stiff and formal, and she hands the phone quickly to Jane.

Today things aren't very busy, and they work a crossword together, making sure to keep it out of sight of the salesmen, who occasionally wander in to waste time with them. Eveline plays her radio and hums along with some of the songs. It's a long, slow day, and when Martin calls Jane feels herself growing anxious—something is moving in the pit of her stomach.

"Are you still mad at me?" he says.

"No," she tells him.

"Say you love me."

"I love you."

"Everybody's asleep here," he says. "I wish you were with me."

She says, "Right."

"I do," he says.

"Okay."

"You don't believe me?"

"I said *okay*."

"Is it busy today?" he asks.

"Not too."

"You're bored, then."

"A little," she says.

"How's the headache?"

"Just the edge of one."

"I'm sorry," he says.

"It's not your fault."

"Sometimes I feel like it is."

"How's *your* head?" she says.

"Terrible."

"Poor boy."

"I wish something would happen around here," he says. "A lot of guys snoring."

"Martin," she says, "I've got to go."

"Okay."

"You want me to stop by tonight?" she asks.

"If you want to."

"Maybe I will."

"You don't have to."

She thinks about him where he is: she imagines him, comfortable, sitting on a couch in front of a television. Sometimes, when nothing's going on, he watches all the soaps. He was hooked on *General Hospital* for a while. That he's her husband seems strange, and she thinks of the nights she's lain in his arms, whispering his name over and over, putting her hands in his hair and rocking with him in the dark. She tells him she loves him, and hangs the phone up. Eveline makes a gesture of frustration and envy.

"Nuts," Eveline says. "Nuts to you and your lovey-dovey stuff."

Jane is sitting in a bath of cold inner light, trying to think of her husband as someone she recognizes.

"Let's do something tonight," Eveline says. "Maybe I'll get lucky."

"I'm not going with you if you're going to be giving strange men the eye," Jane says. She hasn't quite heard herself. She's surprised when Eveline reacts.

"How dare you say a nasty thing like that? I don't know if I want to go out with someone who doesn't think any more of me than *that*."

"I'm sorry," Jane says, patting the other woman's wrist. "I didn't mean anything by it, really. I was just teasing."

"Well, don't tease that way. It hurts my feelings."

"I'm sorry," Jane says again. "Please—really." She feels near crying.

"Well, okay," Eveline says. "Don't get upset. I'm half teasing myself."

Jane sniffles, wipes her eyes with the back of one hand.

"What's wrong, anyway?" Eveline says.

"Nothing," Jane says. "I hurt your feelings."

THAT evening they ride in Eveline's car over to Shakey's for a pizza, and then stroll down to the end of the block, to the new mini-mall on Lincoln Avenue. The night is breezy and warm. A storm is building over the town square. They window-shop for a while, and finally they stop at a new corner café, to sit in a booth by the windows, drinking beer.

Across the street one of the movies has ended, and people are filing out, or waiting around. A few of them head this way.

"They don't look like they enjoyed the movie very much," Eveline says.

"Maybe they did, and they're just depressed to be back in the real world."

"Look, what is it?" Eveline asks suddenly.

Jane returns her gaze.

"What's wrong?"

"Nothing."

"Something's wrong," Eveline says.

Two boys from the high school come past, and one of them winks at Jane. She remembers how it was in high school—the games of flirtation and pursuit, of ignoring some people and noticing others. That seemed like such an unbearable time, and it's already years ago. She watches Eveline light yet another cigarette and feels very much older than her own memory of herself. She sees the person she is now, with Martin, somewhere years away, happy, with children, and with different worries. It's a vivid daydream. She sits there fabricating it, feeling it for what it is and feeling, too, that nothing will change: the Martin she sees in the daydream is nothing like the man she lives with. She thinks of Milly Harmon, pregnant and talking about waiting to be surprised by love.

"I think I'd like to have a baby," she says. She hadn't known she would say it.

Eveline says, "Yuck," blowing smoke.

"Yuck," Jane says. "That's great. Great response, Evie."

They're quiet awhile. Beyond the square the clouds break up into tatters, and lightning strikes out. They hear thunder, and the smell of rain is in the air. The trees in the little park across from the theater move in the wind, and leaves blow out of them.

"Wouldn't you like to have a family?" Jane says.

"Sure."

"Well, the last time I checked, that meant having babies."

"Yuck," Eveline says again.

"Oh, all right—you just mean because of the pain and all."

"I mean yuck."

"Well, what does 'yuck' mean, okay?"

"What *is* the matter with you?" Eveline says. "What difference does it make?"

"I'm trying to have a normal conversation," Jane says, "and I'm getting these weird one-word answers, that's all. I mean what's 'yuck,' anyway? What's it mean?"

"Let's say it means I don't want to talk about having babies."

"I wasn't talking about you."

Each is now a little annoyed with the other. Jane has noticed that whenever she talks about anything that might border on plans for the future, the other woman becomes irritatingly sardonic and closemouthed. Eveline sits there smoking her cigarette and watching the storm come. From beyond the square they hear sirens, which seem to multiply. The whole city seems to be mobilizing. Jane thinks of Martin out there where all those alarms are converging. How odd to know where your husband is by a sound everyone hears. She remembers lying awake nights early in the marriage, hearing sirens and worrying about what might happen. And now, through a slanting sheet of rain, as though something in these thoughts has produced her, Milly Harmon comes, holding an open magazine above her head. She sees Jane and Eveline in the window and waves at them. "Oh, God," Eveline says. "Isn't that Milly Harmon?"

Milly comes into the café and stands for a moment, shaking water from herself. Her hair is wet, as are her shoulders. She pushes her hair away from her forehead, and wipes the rain away with the back of one hand. Then she walks over and says, "Hi, honey," to Jane, bending down to kiss her on the side of the face. Jane manages to seem glad to see her. "You remember my friend Eveline from work," she says.

"I think I do, sure," Milly says.

"Maybe not," Eveline says.

"No, I think I do."

"I have one of those faces that remind you of somebody you never met," Eveline says.

Jane covers this with a laugh as Milly settles on her side of the booth.

Milly is breathless, all bustle and worry, arranging herself, getting comfortable. "Do you hear that?" she says about the sirens. "I swear, it must be a big one. I wish I didn't hear the sirens. It makes me so jumpy and scared. Wally would never forgive me if I did, but I wish I could get up the nerve to go see what it is."

"So," Eveline says, blowing smoke, "how's the baby coming along?"

Milly looks down at herself. "Sleeping now, I think."

"Wally—is it Wally?"

"Wally, yes."

"Wally doesn't let you chase ambulances?"

"I don't chase ambulances."

"Well, I mean—you aren't allowed to go see what's what when you hear sirens?"

"I don't want to see."

"I guess not."

"He's seen some terrible things. They all have. It must be terrible sometimes."

"Right," Eveline says. "It must be terrible."

Milly waves her hand in front of her face. "I wish you wouldn't smoke."

"I was smoking before you came," Eveline says. "I didn't know you were coming."

Milly looks confused for a second. Then she sits back a little and folds her hands on the table. She's chosen to ignore Eveline. She looks at Jane and says, "I had that dream last night."

Jane says, "What dream?"

"That Wally was gone."

Jane says nothing.

"But it wasn't the same, really. He'd left me, you know—the baby was born and he'd just gone off. I was so mad at him. And I had this crying little baby in my lap."

Eveline swallows the last of her beer and then gets up and goes out to stand near the line of wet pavement at the edge of the awninged sidewalk.

"What's the matter with her?" Milly asks.

"She's just unhappy."

"Did I say something wrong?"

"No—really. It's nothing." Jane says.

She pays for the beer. Milly talks to her for a while, but Jane has a hard time concentrating on much of anything now, with sirens going and Eveline standing out there at the edge of the sidewalk. Milly goes on, talking nervously about Wally's leaving her in her dream and how funny it is that she woke up mad at him, that she had to wait a few minutes and get her head clear before she could kiss him good morning.

"I've got to go," Jane says. "I came in Eveline's car."

"Oh, I'm sorry—sure. I just stepped in out of the rain myself."

They join Eveline outside, and Milly says she's got to go get her nephews before they knock down the ice-cream parlor. Jane and Eveline watch her walk away in the rain, and Eveline says, "Jesus."

"She's just scared," Jane says. "God, leave her alone."

"I don't mean anything by it," Eveline says. "A little malice, maybe."

Jane says nothing. They stand there watching the rain and lightning, and soon they're talking about people at work, the salesmen and the boys in the parts shop. They're relaxed now; the sirens have stopped and the tension between them has lifted. They laugh about one salesman who's apparently interested in Eveline. He's a married man—an overweight, balding, middle-aged Texan who wears snakeskin boots and a string tie, and who has an enormous fake-diamond ring on the little finger of his left hand. Eveline calls him Disco Bill. And yet Jane thinks her friend may be secretly attracted to him. She teases her about this, or begins to, and then a clap of thunder so frightens them both that they laugh about it, off and on, through the rest of the evening. They wind up visiting Eveline's parents, who live only a block from the café. Eveline's parents have been married almost thirty years, and, sitting in their living room, Jane looks at their things— the love seat and the antique chairs, the handsome grandfather clock in the hall, the paintings. The place has a lovely *tended* look about it. Everything seems to stand for the kind of life she wants for herself: an attentive, loving husband; children; and a quiet house with a clock that chimes. She knows this is all very dreamy and childish, and yet she looks at Eveline's parents, those people with their almost thirty years' love, and her heart aches. She drinks four glasses of white wine and realizes near the end of the visit that she's talking too much, laughing too loudly.

IT's very late when she gets home. She lets herself in the side door of the house and walks through the rooms, turning on all the lights, as is her custom—she wants to be sure no one is hiding in any of the nooks and crannies. Tonight she looks at everything and feels demeaned by it. Martin's clean uniforms are lying across the back of the lounge chair in the living room. The TV and the TV trays are in one corner, next to the coffee table, which is a gift from Martin's parents, something they bought back in the fifties, before Martin was born. Martin's parents live on a farm ten miles outside town, and for the past year Jane has had to spend Sundays out there, sitting in that living room with its sparse, starved look, listening to Martin's father talk about the weather, or what he had to eat for lunch, or the wrestling matches he watches on TV. He's a kindly man but he has nothing whatever of interest to say, and he seems to know it—his own voice always seems to surprise him at first, as if some profound inner silence had been broken; he pauses, seems to gather himself, and then continues with the considered, slow cadences of oration. He's tall and lean and powerful looking; he wears coveralls, and he reminds Jane of those pictures of hungry, bewildered men in the Dust Bowl thirties—with their sad, straight, combed hair and their desperation. Yet he's a man who seems quite certain about things, quite calm and satisfied. His wife fusses around him, making sure of his comfort, and he speaks to her in exactly the same soft, sure tones he uses with Jane.

Now, sitting in her own living room, thinking about this man, her father-in-law, Jane realizes that she can't stand another Sunday afternoon listening to him talk. It comes to her like a chilly premonition, and quite suddenly, with a kind of tidal shifting inside her, she feels the full weight of her unhappiness. For the first time it seems unbearable, like something that might drive her out of her mind. She breathes, swallows, closes her eyes and opens them. She looks at her own reflection in one of the darkened windows of the kitchen, and then she finds herself in the bedroom, pulling her things out of the closet and throwing them on the bed. Something about this is a little frantic, as though each motion fed some impulse to go further, go through with it—use this night, make her way somewhere else. For a long time she works, getting the clothes out where she can see them. She's lost herself in the practical matter of getting packed. She can't decide what to take, and then she can't find a suitcase or an overnight bag. Finally she settles on one of Martin's travel bags, from when he was in the reserves. She's hurrying, stuffing everything into the bag, and when the bag is almost full she stops, feeling spent and out of breath. She sits down at her dressing table for a moment, and now she wonders if perhaps this is all the result of what she's had to drink. The alcohol is wearing off. She has the beginning of a headache. But she knows that whatever she decides to do should be done in the light of day, not now, at night. At last she gets up from the chair and lies down on the bed to think. She's dizzy. Her mind swims. She can't think, so she remains where she is, lying in the tangle of clothes she hasn't packed yet. Perhaps half an hour goes by. She wonders how long this will go on. And then she's asleep. She's nowhere, not even dreaming.

SHE wakes to the sound of voices. She sits up and tries to get her eyes to focus, tries to open them wide enough to see in the light. The imprint of the wrinkled clothes is in the skin of her face; she can feel it with her fingers. And then she's watching as two men bring Martin in through the front door and help him lie down on the couch. It's all framed in the perspective of the hallway and the open bedroom door, and she's not certain that it's actually happening.

"Martin?" she murmurs, getting up, moving toward them. She stands in the doorway of the living room, rubbing her eyes and trying to clear her head. The two men are standing over her husband, who says something in a pleading voice to one of them. He's lying on his side on the couch, both

hands bandaged, a bruise on the side of his face as if something had spilled there.

"Martin," Jane says.

And the two men move, as if startled by her voice. She
realizes she's never seen them before. One of them, the
younger one, is already explaining. They're from another
company. "We were headed back this way," he says, "and
we thought it'd be better if you didn't hear anything over
the phone." While he talks, the older one is leaning over
Martin, going on about insurance. He's a big square-shoul-
dered man with an extremely rubbery look to his face. Jane
notices this, notices the masklike quality of it, and she begins
to tremble. Everything is oddly exaggerated—something is
being said, they're telling her that Martin burned his hands,
and another voice is murmuring something. Both men go on
talking, apologizing, getting ready to leave her there. She's
not fully awake. The lights in the room hurt her eyes; she
feels a little sick to her stomach. The two men go out on the
porch and then look back through the screen. "You take it
easy, now," the younger one says to Jane. She closes the
door, understands that what she's been hearing under the
flow of the past few moments is Martin's voice muttering her
name, saying something. She walks over to him.

"Jesus," he says. "It's awful. I burned my hands and I
didn't even know it. I didn't even feel it."

She says, "Tell me what happened."

"God," he says. "Wally Harmon's dead. God. I saw it
happen."

"Milly—" she begins. She can't speak.

He's crying. She moves to the entrance of the kitchen and
turns to look at him. "I saw Milly tonight." The room seems
terribly small to her.

"The Van Pickel Lumberyard went up. The warehouse.
Jesus."

She goes into the kitchen and runs water. Outside the window above the sink she sees the dim street, the shadows of houses without light. She drinks part of a glass of water and then pours the rest down the sink. Her throat is still very dry. When she goes back into the living room, she finds him lying on his side, facing the wall.

"Martin?" she says.

"What?"

But she can't find anything to tell him. She says, "God— poor Milly." Then she makes her way into the bedroom and begins putting away the clothes. She doesn't hear him get up, and she's startled to find him standing in the doorway, staring at her.

"What're you doing?" he asks.

She faces him, at a loss—and it's her hesitation that gives him his answer.

"Jane?" he says, looking at the travel bag.

"Look," she tells him, "I had a little too much to drink tonight."

He just stares at her.

"Oh, this," she manages. "I—I was just going through what I have to wear."

But it's too late. "Jesus," he says, turning from her a little.

"Martin," she says.

"What."

"Does—did somebody tell Milly?"

He nods. "Teddy. Teddy stayed with her. She was crazy. Crazy."

He looks at his hands. It's as if he just remembered them. They're wrapped tight; they look like two white clubs. "Jesus, Jane, are you—" He stops, shakes his head. "Jesus."

"Don't," she says.

"Without even talking to me about it—"

"Martin, this is not the time to talk about anything."

He's quiet a moment, standing there in the doorway. "I

keep seeing it," he says. "I keep seeing Wally's face. The—the way his foot jerked. His foot jerked like with electricity and he was—oh, Christ, he was already dead."

"Oh, don't," she says. "Please. Don't talk. Stop picturing it."

"They gave me something to make me sleep," he says. "And I won't sleep." He wanders back into the living room. A few minutes later she goes to him there and finds that whatever the doctors gave him has worked. He's lying on his back, and he looks smaller somehow, his bandaged hands on his chest, his face pinched with grief, with whatever he's dreaming. He twitches and mutters something and moans. She turns the light off and tiptoes back to the bedroom. She's the one who won't sleep. She gets into the bed and huddles there, leaving the light on. Outside the wind gets up—another storm rolls in off the plains. She listens as the rain begins, and hears the far-off drumming of thunder. The whole night seems deranged. She thinks of Wally Harmon, dead out in the blowing, rainy dark. And then she remembers Milly and her bad dreams, how she looked coming from the downpour, the wet street, with the magazine held over her head—her body so rounded, so weighted down with her baby, her love, the love she had waited for, that she said had surprised her. These events are too much to think about, too awful to imagine. The world seems cruelly immense now, and remorselessly itself. When Martin groans in the other room, she wishes he'd stop, and then she imagines that it's another time, that she's just awakened from a dream and is trying to sleep while they all sit in her living room and talk the hours of the night away.

IN the morning she's awake first. She gets up and wraps herself in a robe and then shuffles into the kitchen and puts coffee on. For a minute it's like any other morning. She sits at the table to wait for the coffee water to boil. He comes in like someone entering a stranger's kitchen—his movements are tentative, almost shy. She's surprised to see that he's still in his uniform. He says, "I need you to help me go to the bathroom. I can't get my pants undone." He starts trying to work his belt loose.

"Wait," she says. "Here, hold on."

"I have to get out of these clothes, Jane. I think they smell like smoke."

"Let me do it," she says.

"Milly's in the hospital—they had to put her under sedation."

"Move your hands out of the way," Jane says to him.

She has to help with everything, and when the time comes for him to eat, she has to feed him. She spoons scrambled eggs into his mouth and holds the coffee cup to his lips, and when that's over with, she wipes his mouth and chin with a damp napkin. Then she starts bathwater running and helps him out of his underclothes. They work silently, and with a kind of embarrassment, until he's sitting down and the water is right. When she begins to run a soapy rag over his back, he utters a small sound of satisfaction and comfort. But then he's crying again. He wants to talk about Wally Harmon's death. He says he has to. He tells her that a piece of hot metal the size of an arrow dropped from the roof of the Van Pickel warehouse and hit poor Wally Harmon in the top of the back.

"It didn't kill him right away," he says, sniffling. "Oh, Jesus. He looked right at me and asked if I thought he'd be all right. We were talking about it, honey. He reached up— he—over his shoulder. He took ahold of it for a second. Then he—then he looked at me and said he could feel it down in his stomach."

"Don't think about it," Jane says.

"Oh, God." He's sobbing. "God."

"Martin, honey—"

"I've done the best I could," he says. "Haven't I?"

"Shhh," she says, bringing the warm rag over his shoulders and wringing it, so that the water runs down his back.

They're quiet again. Together they get him out of the tub, and then she dries him off, helps him into a pair of jeans.

"Thanks," he says, not looking at her. Then he says, "Jane."

She's holding his shirt out for him, waiting for him to turn and put his arms into the sleeves. She looks at him.

"Honey," he says.

"I'm calling in," she tells him. "I'll call Eveline. We'll go be with Milly."

"Last night," he says.

She looks straight at him.

He hesitates, glances down. "I—I'll try and do better." He seems about to cry again. For some reason this makes her feel abruptly very irritable and nervous. She turns from him, walks into the living room and begins putting the sofa back in order. When he comes to the doorway and says her name, she doesn't answer, and he walks through to the kitchen door.

"What're you doing?" she says to him.

"Can you give me some water?"

She moves into the kitchen and he follows her. She runs water, to get it cold, and he stands at her side. When the glass is filled, she holds it to his mouth. He swallows, and she takes the glass away. "If you want to talk about any-thing—" he says.

"Why don't you try to sleep awhile?" she says.

He says, "I know I've been talking about Wally—"

"Just please—go lie down or something."

"When I woke up this morning, I remembered everything, and I thought you might be gone."

"Well, I'm not gone."

"I knew we were having some trouble, Jane—"

"Just let's not talk about it now," she says. "All right? I have to go call Eveline." She walks into the bedroom, and when he comes in behind her she tells him very gently to please go get off his feet. He backs off, makes his way into the living room. "Can you turn on the television?" he calls to her.

She does so. "What channel do you want?"

"Can you just go through them a little?"

She's patient. She waits for him to get a good look at each channel. There isn't any news coverage; it's all commercials and cartoons and children's shows. Finally he settles on a rerun of *The Andy Griffith Show*, and she leaves him there. She fills the dishwasher and wipes off the kitchen table. Then she calls Eveline to tell her what's happened.

"You poor thing," Eveline says. "You must be so relieved. And I said all that bad stuff about Wally's wife."

Jane says, "You didn't mean it," and suddenly she's crying. She's got the handset held tight against her face, crying.

"You poor thing," Eveline says. "You want me to come over there?"

"No, it's all right—I'm all right."

"Poor Martin. Is he hurt bad?"

"It's his hands."

"Is it very painful?"

"Yes," Jane says.

LATER, while he sleeps on the sofa, she wanders outside and walks down to the end of the driveway. The day is sunny and cool, with little cottony clouds—the kind of clear day that comes after a storm. She looks up and down the street.

Nothing is moving. A few houses away someone has put up a flag, and it flutters in a stray breeze. This is the way it was, she remembers, when she first lived here—when she first stood on this sidewalk and marveled at how flat the land was, how far it stretched in all directions. Now she turns and makes her way back to the house, and then she finds herself in the garage. It's almost as if she's saying good-bye to everything, and as this thought occurs to her, she feels a little stir of sadness. Here on the worktable, side by side under the light from the one window, are Martin's model airplanes. He won't be able to work on them again for weeks. The light reveals the miniature details, the crevices and curves on which he lavished such care, gluing and sanding and painting. The little engines are lying on a paper towel at one end of the table; they smell just like real engines, and they're shiny with lubrication. She picks one of them up and turns it in the light, trying to understand what he might see in it that could require such time and attention. She wants to understand him. She remembers that when they dated, he liked to tell her about flying these planes, and his eyes would widen with excitement. She remembers that she liked him best when he was glad that way. She puts the little engine down, thinking how people change. She knows she's going to leave him, but just for this moment, standing among these things, she feels almost peaceful about it. There's no need to hurry. As she steps out on the lawn, she realizes she can take the time to think clearly about when and where; she can even change her mind. But she doesn't think she will.

He's up. He's in the hallway—he had apparently wakened and found her gone. "Jesus," he says. "I woke up and you weren't here."

"I didn't go anywhere," she says, and she smiles at him.

"I'm sorry," he says, starting to cry. "God, Janey, I'm so sorry. I'm all messed up here. I've got to go to the bathroom again."

She helps him. The two of them stand over the bowl. He's stopped crying now, though he says his hands hurt something awful. When he's finished he thanks her, and then tries a bawdy joke. "You don't have to let go so soon."

She ignores this, and when she has him tucked safely away, he says quietly, "I guess I better just go to bed and sleep some more if I can."

She's trying to hold on to the feeling of peace and certainty she had in the garage. It's not even noon, and she's exhausted. She's very tired of thinking about everything. He's talking about his parents; later she'll have to call them. But then he says he wants his mother to hear his voice first, to know he's all right. He goes on—something about Milly and her unborn baby, and Teddy Lynch—but Jane can't quite hear him: he's a little unsteady on his feet, and they have trouble negotiating the hallway together.

In their bedroom she helps him out of his jeans and shirt, and she actually tucks him into the bed. Again he thanks her. She kisses his forehead, feels a sudden, sick-swooning sense of having wronged him somehow. It makes her stand straighter, makes her stiffen slightly.

"Jane?" he says.

She breathes. "Try to rest some more. You just need to rest now." He closes his eyes and she waits a little. He's not asleep. She sits at the foot of the bed and watches him. Perhaps ten minutes go by. Then he opens his eyes.

"Janey?"

"Shhh," she says.

He closes them again. It's as if he were her child. She thinks of him as he was when she first saw him, tall and sure of himself in his uniform, and the image makes her throat constrict.

At last he's asleep. When she's certain of this, she lifts herself from the bed and carefully, quietly withdraws. As she closes the door, something in the flow of her own mind appalls her, and she stops, stands in the dim hall-way, frozen in a kind of wonder: she had been thinking in an abstract way, almost idly, as though it had nothing at all to do with her, about how people will go to such lengths leaving a room—wishing not to disturb, not to awaken, a loved one.

CONSOLATION

LATE one summer afternoon, Milly Harmon and her older sister, Meg, spend a blessed, uncomplicated hour at a motel pool in Philadelphia, sitting in the shade of one of the big umbrella tables. They drink tropical punch from cans, and Milly nurses the baby, staring out at the impossibly silver agitation of water around the body of a young, dark swimmer, a boy with Spanish black hair and eyes. He's the only one in the pool. Across the way, an enormous woman in a red terry-cloth bikini lies on her stomach in the sun, her head resting on her folded arms. Milly's sister puts her own head down for a moment, then looks at Milly. "I feel fat," she says, low. "I look like that woman over there, I just know it."

"Be quiet," Milly says. "Your voice carries."

"Nobody can hear us," Meg says. She's always worried about weight, though she's nothing like the woman across the way. Her thighs are heavy, her hips wide, but she's big-boned, as their mother always says; she's not built to be skinny. Milly's the one who's skinny. When they were growing up, Meg often called her "stick." Sometimes it was an endearment and sometimes it was a jibe, depending on the circumstances. These days, Meg calls her "honey" and speaks to her with something like the careful tones of sympathy. Milly's husband was killed last September, when Milly was almost six months pregnant, and the two women have traveled here to see Milly's in-laws, to show them their grandchild, whom they have never seen.

The visit hasn't gone well. Things have been strained and awkward. Milly is exhausted and discouraged, so her sister has worked everything out, making arrangements for the evening, preserving these few hours in the day for the two of them and the baby. In a way, the baby's the problem: Milly would never have suspected that her husband's parents would react so peevishly, with such annoyance, to their only grandson—the only grandchild they will ever have.

Last night, when the baby started crying at dinner, both the Harmons seemed to sulk, and finally Wally's father excused himself and went to bed—went into his bedroom and turned a radio on. His dinner was still steaming on his plate; they hadn't even quite finished passing the food around. The music sounded through the walls of the small house, while Milly, Wally's mother and Meg sat through the meal trying to be cordial to each other, the baby fussing between them.

Finally Wally's mother said, "Perhaps if you nurse him."

"I just did," Milly told her.

"Well, he wants *something*."

"Babies cry," Meg put in, and the older woman looked at her as though she had said something off-color.

"Hush," Milly said to the baby. "Be quiet." Then there seemed nothing left to say.

Mrs. Harmon's hands trembled over the lace edges of the tablecloth. "Can I get you anything?" she said.

At the end of the evening she took Milly by the elbow and murmured, "I'm afraid you'll have to forgive us, we're just not used to the commotion."

"Commotion," Meg said as they drove back to the motel. "Jesus. Commotion."

Milly looked down into the sleeping face of her son. "My little commotion," she said, feeling tired and sad.

* * *

Now Meg turns her head on her arms and gazes at the boy in the pool. "Maybe I'll go for a swim," she says.

"He's too young for you," Milly says.

Meg affects a forlorn sigh, then sits straight again. "You want me to take Zeke for a while?" The baby's name is Wally, after his dead father, but Meg calls him Zeke. She claims she's always called every baby Zeke, boy or girl, but she's especially fond of the name for *this* baby. This baby, she says, looks like a Zeke. Even Milly uses the name occasionally, as an endearment.

"He's not through nursing," Milly says.

It's been a hot day. Even now, at almost six o'clock, the sky is pale blue and crossed with thin, fleecy clouds that look like filaments of steam. Meg wants a tan, or says she does, but she's worn a kimono all afternoon, and hasn't moved out of the shade. She's with Milly these days because her marriage is breaking up. It's an amicable divorce; there are no children. Meg says the whole thing simply collapsed of its own weight. Neither party is interested in anyone else, and there haven't been any ugly scenes or secrets. They just don't want to be married to each other anymore, see no future in it. She talks about how civilized the whole procedure has been, how even the lawyers are remarking on it, but Milly thinks she hears some sorrow in her voice. She thinks of two friends of hers who have split up twice since the warehouse fire that killed Wally, and whose explanations, each time, have seemed to preclude any possibility of reconciliation. Yet they're now living together, and sometimes, when Milly sees them, they seem happy.

"Did I tell you that Jane and Martin are back together?" she asks Meg.

"Again?"

She nods.

"Tied to each other on a rock in space," Meg says.

"What?"

"Come on, let me hold Zeke," Meg reaches for the baby. "He's through, isn't he?"

"He's asleep."

Meg pretends to pout, extending her arm across the table and putting her head down again. She makes a yawning sound. "Where are all the boys? Let's have some fun here anyway—right? Let's get in a festive mood or something."

Milly removes the baby's tight little sucking mouth from her breast and covers herself. The baby sleeps on, still sucking. "Look at this," she says to her sister.

Meg leans toward her to see. "What in the world do you think is wrong with them?"

She's talking about Wally's parents, of course. Milly shrugs. She doesn't feel comfortable discussing them. She wants the baby to have both sets of grandparents, and a part of her feels that this ambition is in some way laudatory— that the strange, stiff people she has brought her child all this way to see ought to appreciate what she's trying to do. She wonders if they harbor some resentment about how before she would marry their son she'd extracted a promise from him about not leaving Illinois, where her parents and her sister live. It's entirely possible that Wally's parents unconsciously blame her for Wally's death, for the fact that his body lies far away in her family's plot in a cemetery in Lincoln, Illinois.

"Hey," Meg says.

"What."

"I asked a question. You drove all the way out here to see them and let them see their grandson, and they act like it's some kind of bother."

"They're just tired," Milly says. "Like we are."

"Seven hundred miles of driving to sit by a motel pool."

"They're not used to having a baby around," Milly says. "It's awkward for them, too." She wishes her sister would stop. "Can't we just not worry it all to death?"

"Hey," Meg says. "It's your show."

Milly says, "We'll see them tonight and then we'll leave in the morning and that'll be that, okay?"

"I wonder what they're doing right now. You think they're watching the four o'clock movie or something? With their only grandson two miles away in a motel?"

In a parking lot in front of a group of low buildings on the other side of the highway, someone sets off a pack of firecrackers—they make a sound like small machine-gun fire.

"All these years of independence," Meg says. "So people like us can have these wonderful private lives."

Milly smiles. It's always been Meg who defined things, who spoke out and offered opinions. Milly thinks of her sister as someone who knows the world, someone with experience she herself lacks, though Meg is only a little more than a year older. So much of her own life seems somehow duplicitous to her, as if the wish to please others and to be well thought of had somehow dulled the edges of her identity and left her with nothing but a set of received impressions. She knows she loves the baby in her lap, and she knows she loved her husband—though during the four years of her marriage she was confused much of the time, and afraid of her own restlessness. It was only in the weeks just before Wally was taken from her that she felt most comfortably in love with him, glad of his presence in the house and worried about the dangerous fire-fighting work that was, in fact, the agency of his death. She doesn't want to think about this now, and she marvels at how a moment of admiration for the expressiveness of her sister could lead to remembering that her husband died just as she was beginning to understand her need for him. She draws a little shuddering breath, and Meg frowns.

"You looked like something hurt you," Meg says. "You were thinking about Wally."

Milly nods.

"Zeke looks like him, don't you think?"

"I wasted so much time wondering if I loved him," Milly says.

"I think he was happy," her sister tells her.

In the pool the boy splashes and dives, disappears; Milly watches the shimmery surface. He comes up on the other side, spits a stream of water, and climbs out. He's wearing tight, dark blue bathing trunks.

"Come on," Meg says, reaching for the baby. "Let me have him."

"I don't want to wake him," Milly says.

Meg walks over to the edge of the pool, takes off her sandals, and dips the toe of one foot in, as though trying to gauge how cold the water is. She comes back, sits down, drops the sandals between her feet and steps into them one by one. "You know what I think it is with the Harmons?" she says. "I think it's the war. I think the war got them. That whole generation."

Milly ignores this, and adjusts, slightly, the weight of the baby in her lap. "Zeke," she says. "Pretty Zeke."

The big woman across the way has labored up off her towel and is making slow progress out of the pool area.

"Wonder if she's married," Meg says. "I think I'll have a pool party when the divorce is final."

The baby stirs in Milly's lap. She moves slightly, rocking her legs.

"We ought to live together permanently," Meg says.

"You want to keep living with us?"

"Sure, why not? Zeke and I get along. A divorced woman and a widow. And one cool baby boy."

They're quiet a while. Somewhere off beyond the trees at the end of the motel parking lot, more firecrackers go off. Meg stands, stretches. "I knew a guy once who swore he got drunk and slept on top of the Tomb of the Unknown Soldier. On Independence Day. Think of it."

"You didn't believe him," Milly says.

"I believed he had the idea. Whole culture's falling apart. Whole goddamn thing."

"Do you really want to stay with us?" Milly asks her.

"I don't know. That's an idea, too." She ambles over to the pool again, then walks around it, out of the gate, to the small stairway leading up to their room. At the door of the room she turns, shrugs, seems to wait. Milly lifts the baby to her shoulder, then rises. Meg is standing at the railing on the second level, her kimono partway open at the legs. Milly, approaching her, thinks she looks wonderful, and tells her so.

"I was just standing here wondering how long it'll take to drive you crazy if we keep living together," Meg says, opening the door to the room. Inside, in the air-conditioning, she flops down on the nearest bed. Milly puts the baby in the Port-a-Crib and turns to see that the telephone message light is on. "Hey, look," she says.

Meg says, "Ten to one it's the Harmons canceling out."

"No bet," Milly says, tucking the baby in. "Oh, I just want to go home, anyway."

Her sister dials the front desk, then sits cross-legged with pillows at her back, listening. "I don't believe this," she says.

IT turns out that there are two calls: one from the Harmons, who say they want to come earlier than planned, and one from Meg's estranged husband, Larry, who has apparently traveled here from Champaign, Illinois. When Meg calls the number he left, he answers, and she waves Milly out of the room. Milly takes the baby, who isn't quite awake, and walks back down to the pool. It's empty; the water is perfectly smooth. She sits down, watches the light shift on the surface, clouds moving across it in reflection.

It occurs to her that she might have to spend the rest of the trip on her own, and this thought causes a flutter at the pit of her stomach. She thinks of Larry, pulling this stunt, and she wonders why she didn't imagine that he might show up, her sister's casual talk of the divorce notwithstanding. He's always been prone to the grand gesture: once, after a particularly bad quarrel, he rented a van with loudspeakers and drove up and down the streets of Champaign, proclaiming his love. Milly remembers this, sitting by the empty pool, and feels oddly threatened.

It isn't long before Meg comes out and calls her back. Meg is already trying to make herself presentable. What Larry wants, she tells Milly, what he pleaded for, is only that Meg agree to see him. He came to Philadelphia and began calling all the Harmons in the phone book, and when he got Wally's parents, they gave him the number of the motel. "The whole thing's insane," she says, hurriedly brushing her hair. "I don't get it. We're almost final."

"Meg, I need you now," Milly says.

"Don't be ridiculous," says her sister.

"What're we going to do about the Harmons?"

"Larry says they asked him to say hello to you. Can you feature that? I mean, what in the world is that? It's like they don't expect to see you again."

"Yes," Milly says. "But they're coming."

"He called before, you know."

"Mr. Harmon?"

"No—Larry. He called just before we left. I didn't get it. I mean, he kept hinting around and I just didn't get it. I guess I told him we were coming to Philly."

The baby begins to whine and complain.

"Hey, Zeke," Meg says. She looks in the mirror. "Good Lord, I look like war," and then she's crying. She moves to the bed, sits down, still stroking her hair with the brush.

"Don't cry," Milly says. "You don't want to look all red-eyed, do you?"

"What the hell," Meg says. "I'm telling you, I don't care about it. I mean—I don't care. He's such a baby about everything."

Milly is completely off balance. She has been the one in need on this trip, and now everything's turned around. "Here," she says, offering her sister a Kleenex. "You can't let him see you looking miserable."

"You believe this?" Meg says. "You think I should go with him?"

"He wants to take you somewhere?"

"I don't know."

"What about the Harmons?"

Meg looks at her. "What about them?"

"They're on their way here, too."

"I can't handle the Harmons anymore," Meg tells her.

"Who asked you to handle them?"

"You know what I mean."

"Well—are you just going to go off with Larry?"

"I don't know what he wants."

"Well, for God's sake, Meg. He wouldn't come all this way just to tell you hello."

"That's what he said. He said 'Hello.' "

"*Meg.*"

"I'm telling you, honey, I just don't have a clue."

IN a little while Larry arrives, looking sheepish and expectant. Milly lets him in, and accepts his clumsy embrace, explaining that Meg is in the bathroom changing out of her bathing suit.

"Hey," he says, "I brought mine with me."

"She'll be through in a minute."

"Is she mad at me?" he asks.

"She's just changing," Milly tells him.

He looks around the room, walks over to the Port-a-Crib and stands there making little cooing sounds at the baby. "He's smiling at me. Look at that."

"He smiles a lot." She moves to the other side of the crib and watches him make funny faces at the baby.

Larry is a fair, willowy man, and though he's older than Milly, she has always felt a tenderness toward him for his obvious unease with her, for the way Meg orders him around, and for his boyish romantic fragility—which, she realizes now, reminds her a little of Wally. It's in the moment that she wishes he hadn't come here that she thinks of this, and abruptly she has an urge to reach across the crib and touch his wrist, as if to make up for some wrong she's done. He leans down and puts one finger into the baby's hand. "Look at that," he says. "Quite a grip. Boy's going to be a linebacker."

"He's small for his age," Milly tells him.

"It's not the size. It's the strength."

She says nothing. She wishes Meg would come out of the bathroom. Larry pats the baby's forehead, then moves to the windows and, holding the drapes back, looks out.

"Pretty," he says. "Looks like it'll be a nice, clear night for fireworks."

For the past year or so, Larry has worked in a shoe store in Urbana, and he's gone through several other jobs, though he often talks about signing up for English courses at the junior college and getting started on a career. He wants to save money for school, but in five years he hasn't managed to save enough for one course. He explains himself in terms of his appetite for life: he's unable to put off the present, and frugality sometimes suffers. Meg has often talked about him with a kind of wonder at his capacity for pleasure. It's not a thing she would necessarily want to change. He can make her laugh, and he writes poems to her, to women in general, though according to Meg they're not very good poems.

The truth is, he's an amiable, dreamy young man without an ounce of objectivity about himself, and what he wears on this occasion seems to illustrate this. His bohemian dress is embarrassingly like a costume—the bright red scarf and black beret and jeans; the sleeveless turtleneck shirt, its dark colors bleeding into each other across the front.

"So," he says, turning from the windows. "Are the grand-parents around?"

She draws in a breath, deciding to tell him about the Harmons, but Meg comes out of the bathroom at last. She's wearing the kimono open, showing the white shorts and blouse she's changed into.

Larry stands straight, clears his throat. "God, Meg. You look great," he says.

Meg flops down on the bed nearest the door and lights a cigarette. "Larry, what're you trying to pull here?"

"Nothing," he says. He hasn't moved. He's standing by the windows. "I just wanted to see you again. I thought Philadelphia on the Fourth might be good."

"Okay," Meg says, drawing on the cigarette.

"You know me," he says. "I have a hard time saying this sort of stuff up close."

"What sort of stuff, Larry."

"I'll take Zeke for a walk," Milly says.

"I can't believe this," Meg says, blowing smoke.

Milly gathers up the baby, but Larry stops her. "You don't have to go."

"Stay," Meg tells her.

"I thought I'd go out and meet the Harmons."

"Come on, tell me what you're doing here," Meg says to Larry.

"You don't know?"

"What if I need you to tell me anyway," she says.

He hesitates, then reaches into his jeans and brings out a piece of folded paper. "Here."

Meg takes it, but doesn't open it.

"Aren't you going to read it?"

"I can't read it with you watching me like that. Jesus, Larry—what in the world's going through your mind?"

"I started thinking about it being final," he says, looking down. Milly moves to the other side of the room, to her own bed, still holding the baby.

"I won't read it with you standing here," Meg says.

Larry reaches for the door. "I'll be outside," he says.

Milly, turning to sit with her back to them, hears the door close quietly. She looks at Meg, who's sitting against the headboard of the other bed, the folded paper in her lap.

"Aren't you going to read it?"

"I'm embarrassed for him."

Milly recalls her own, secret, embarrassment at the un-attractive, hyena-like note poor Wally struck every time he laughed. "It was probably done with love," she says.

Meg offers her the piece of paper across the space between the two beds. "You read it to me."

"I can't do that, Meg. It's private. I shouldn't even be here."

Meg opens the folded paper, and reads silently. "Jesus," she says. "Listen to this."

"Meg," Milly says.

"You're my sister. Listen. 'When I began to think our time was really finally up/ My chagrined regretful eyes lumbered tightly shut.' Lumbered, for God's sake."

Milly says nothing.

"My eyes lumbered shut."

And quite suddenly the two of them are laughing. They laugh quietly, or they try to. Milly sets Zeke down on his back, and pulls the pillows of the bed to her face in an attempt to muffle herself, and when she looks up she sees Meg on all fours with her blanket pulled over her head and, beyond her, Larry's faint shadow through the window drapes. He's pacing. He stops and leans on the railing, looking out at the pool.

"Shhh," Meg says, finally. "There's more." She sits straight, composes herself, pushes the hair back from her face, and holds up the now crumpled piece of paper. "Oh," she says. "Ready?"

"Meg, he's right there."

Meg looks. "He can't hear anything."

"Whisper," Milly says.

Meg reads. " 'I cried and sighed under the lids of these lonely eyes/ Because I knew I'd miss your lavish thighs.' "

For a few moments they can say nothing. Milly, coughing and sputtering into the cotton smell of the sheets, has a moment of perceiving, by contrast, the unhappiness she's lived with these last few months, how bad it has been—this terrible time—and it occurs to her that she's managed it long enough not to notice it, quite. Everything is suffused in an ache she's grown accustomed to, and now it's as if she's flying in the face of it all. She laughs more deeply than she ever has, laughs even as she thinks of the Harmons, and of her grief. She's woozy from lack of air and breath. At last she sits up, wipes her eyes with part of the pillowcase, still laughing. The baby's fussing, so she works to stop, to gain some control of herself. She realizes that Meg is in the bathroom, running water. Then Meg comes out and offers her a wet washcloth.

"I didn't see you go in there."

"Quiet," Meg says. "Don't get me started again."

Milly holds the baby on one arm. "I have to feed Zeke some more."

"So once more I don't get to hold him."

They look at each other.

"Poor Larry," Meg says. "Married to a philistine. But—just maybe—he did the right thing, coming here."

"You don't suppose he heard us."

"I don't suppose it matters if he did. He'd never believe we could laugh at one of his *poems*."

"Oh, Meg—that's so mean."

"It's the truth. There are some things, honey, that love just won't change."

Now it's as if they are both suddenly aware of another context for these words—both thinking about Wally. They gaze at each other. But then the moment passes. They turn to the window and Meg says, "Is Larry out there? What'll I tell him anyway?" She crosses the room and looks through the little peephole in the door. "God," she says, "the Harmons are here."

MRS. Harmon is standing in front of the door with Larry, who has apparently begun explaining himself. Larry turns and takes Meg by the arm as she and Milly come out. "All the way from Champaign to head it off," he says to Mrs. Harmon. "I hope I just avoided making the biggest mistake of my life."

"God," Meg says to him. "If only you had money." She laughs at her own joke. Mrs. Harmon steps around her to take the baby's hand. She looks up at Milly. "I'm afraid we went overboard," she says. "We went shopping for the baby."

Milly nods at her. There's confusion now: Larry and Meg are talking, seem about to argue. Larry wants to know what Meg thinks of the poem, but Milly doesn't hear what she says to him. Mrs. Harmon is apologizing for coming earlier than planned.

"It's only an hour or so," Milly says, and then wonders if

that didn't sound somehow ungracious. She can't think of anything else to say. And then she turns to see Mr. Harmon laboring up the stairs. He's carrying a giant teddy bear with a red ribbon wrapped around its thick middle. He has it over his shoulder, like a man lugging a body. The teddy bear is bigger than he is, and the muscles of his neck are straining as he sets it down. "This is for Wally," he says with a smile that seems sad. His eyes are moist. He puts one arm around his wife's puffy midriff and says, "I mean—if it's okay."

"I don't want to be divorced," Larry is saying to Meg.

Milly looks at the Harmons, at the hopeful, nervous expressions on their faces, and then she tries to give them the satisfaction of her best appreciation: she marvels at the size and the softness of the big teddy, and she holds the baby up to it, saying, "See? See?"

"It's quite impractical, of course," says Mr. Harmon.

"We couldn't pass it up," his wife says. "We have some other things in the car."

"I don't know where we'll put it," says Milly.

"We can keep it here," Mrs. Harmon hurries to say. She's holding on to her husband, and her pinched, unhappy features make her look almost frightened. Mr. Harmon raises the hand that had been around her waist and lightly, reassuringly, clasps her shoulder. He stands there, tall and straight in that intentionally ramrod-stiff way of his—the stance, he would say, of an old military man, which happens to be exactly what he is. His wife stands closer to him, murmurs something about the fireworks going off in the distance. It seems to Milly that they're both quite changed; it's as if they've come with bad news and are worried about hurting her with more of it. Then she realizes what it is they are trying to give her, in what is apparently the only way they know how, and she remembers that they have been attempting to get used to the loss of their only child. She feels her throat constrict, and when Larry reaches for her sister, putting his long, boy's arms around Meg, it's as if this embrace is somehow the expression of what they all feel. The Harmons are gazing at the baby now. Still arm in arm.

"Yes," Milly tells them, her voice trembling. "Yes, of course. You—we could keep it here."

Meg and Larry are leaning against the railing, in their embrace. It strikes Milly that she's the only one of these people without a lover, without someone to stand with. She lifts the baby to her shoulder and looks away from them all, but only for a moment. Far off, the sky is turning dusky; it's getting near the time for rockets and exploding blooms of color.

"Dinner for everyone," Mr. Harmon says, his voice full of brave cheerfulness. He leans close to Milly, and speaks to the child. "And you, young fellow, you'll have to wait awhile."

"We'll eat at the motel restaurant and then watch the fireworks," says Mrs. Harmon. "We could sit right here on the balcony and see it all."

Meg touches the arm of the teddy bear. "Thing's as big as a *real* bear," she says.

"I feel like fireworks," Larry says.

"They put on quite a show," says Mr. Harmon. "There used to be a big field out this way—before they widened the street. Big field of grass, and people would gather—"

"We brought Wally here when he was a little boy," Mrs. Harmon says. "So many—such good times."

"They still put on a good show," Mr. Harmon says, squeezing his wife's shoulder.

Milly faces him, faces them, fighting back any sadness. In the next moment, without quite thinking about it, she steps forward slightly and offers her child to Mrs. Harmon. Mrs. Harmon tries to speak, but can't. Her husband clears his throat, lifts the big teddy bear as if to show it to everyone again. But he, too, is unable to speak. He sets it down, and seems momentarily confused. Milly lightly grasps his arm above the elbow, and steps forward to watch her mother-in-law cradle the baby. Mrs. Harmon makes a slight swinging motion, looking at her husband, and then at Milly. "Such a pretty baby," she says.

Mr. Harmon says, "A handsome baby."

Meg and Larry move closer. They all stand there on the motel balcony with the enormous teddy bear propped against the railing. They are quiet, almost shy, not quite looking at each other, and for the moment it's as if, like the crowds beginning to gather on the roofs of the low buildings across the street, they have come here only to wait for what will soon be happening in every quarter of the city of brotherly love.

THE BRACE

TONIGHT, a little more than a month after my one brother turns up out of the blue—ten years older and looking it, with a badly mangled arm from a bomb blast at a church in Beirut—our difficult and famous father arrives from Italy, on yet another of his unannounced stopovers. He calls from the airport to say he's hired a cab and is coming. This time, he says, he's headed back to Santa Monica, having spent the last four months in Rome. When I'm through talking to him, I give the handset to my husband, who puts it back in its cradle and then gives me a look. We smile. Daddy doesn't know James has been staying with us. James is in town somewhere and doesn't know the old man's breezed in. "This is going to be something," I say.

A little later we watch the old man climb out of the cab and work to get his luggage from the trunk. When my husband moves to go out and help him, I take his arm above the elbow. "Tom," I say. "Wait. Let the cabbie do it."

We stand there, the welcoming committee, and I'm thinking how I'll choose the moment to tell my father that his son is visiting, too.

Tom holds the door open, and I step out.

"Don't say anything," I say. "Let me do the talking."

"You're enjoying this too much," Tom says. "I don't think you should get such pleasure out of it."

"It's a reunion," I say, and I think I sound bitter.

"Oh," he says. "Wicked," smiling at me.

Daddy fumbles around in the pockets of his suit while we watch from the porch. "All right," I say. "But watch him make us pay for the cab. Again."

"Listen to you. You can't keep the admiration out of your voice," Tom says. A moment later he says, "I hope we can think of this as a positive thing. Maybe we ought to let them both just stumble onto each other."

"I'd like to film it," I say, and Tom shakes his head.

My father's coming up the walk now, and the cabdriver's leaning against the idling taxi, obviously waiting for his fare. It's getting toward dusk, and there are shadows out in the street. Above the trees I can see the faint outline of the moon, and I think of convergences, chance meetings, and how my father will think I somehow arranged the whole thing. He'll probably blame me for not telling him over the telephone so he could choose to travel on.

"Hey," he says, stepping up onto the porch. His step is slow, and he seems to sag. He looks sleepless and worn out, and there's a faintly jaundiced cast to his skin, a darkness around the eyes. Apparently travel doesn't agree with him the way it used to. It's as if he's not coming from Europe and all sorts of honors and interviews—and a long, successful run of one of his plays—but from a job he hates and has to go back to.

And I'm about to tell him James has come home. They haven't spoken in almost twenty years, since long before James dropped out of sight altogether.

I stand aside and pull the screen open for him and smile, thinking I'll tell him before he says anything. But then I find I can't do it yet. The time is just not right; to say anything now would be somehow aggressive. I myself haven't seen him in more than a year. "Marilyn," he says. And then he nods at Tom. "Tom." For a moment it's like all the other times, and I hear the something condescending in his voice as he says Tom's name, as if the man I chose to marry was a little boy with dirt on his face. Tom takes his bags and starts upstairs with them.

"I need some change to pay the driver," my father says.

"I don't know why you insist on the taxi," Tom says. "I'd pick you up."

"Wouldn't want to trouble you, Tom." My father smiles, all affability and consideration. He told me once that he respects Tom for the fact that Tom isn't capable of understanding what he does and is therefore not in awe of it. He meant it as a compliment, I'm afraid; it was one of his careless observations. He has never been a man with much access to his effect on other people, for all the famous sensibility of the plays.

Now, I give him a twenty-dollar bill and watch him go out to pay the cabbie. He comes back with a five and hands it to me.

"I'll pay you back."

"Don't be silly," I say.

"Don't I get a hug?" he says. I hug him. He smells of cigar smoke. His shoulder, when I touch it, is slack: there's only bone under the skin. I put my lips to his cheek, and he pats my arm, turning a little, as if already looking for a way out. In spite of everything, and regardless of what you might've read or heard about him, my father is essentially a timid man. I can see that he's uneasy, and it makes me sorry for my own thoughts.

"Got to sit down," he says.

"How long can you stay this time?" Tom wants to know.

"Just a day or two. I have to get back home to work."

"What are you working on?" Tom asks him, heading for the kitchen and the drinks.

"Another play. What else?"

"What's it about?" I ask.

He looks at me. He knows something's up now. He smiles and says, "The usual troublesome stuff."

"Can't I be curious about it?" I say.

"It's just that this is slightly out of character for you, isn't it?" he says.

"I don't know what you mean," I tell him.

We're moving into the living room. I've put mints in a glass bowl on the coffee table, and fruits and cheeses on a big platter. It's just the kind of thing about which he has always found something disparaging to say. He seems to appreciate it now, lifting a strawberry and putting it, whole, into his mouth.

"What's the title of the new play?" I ask him.

He says, "*1951*," giving me another look. Nineteen fifty-one is the year my mother died. "It's not about her," he adds. "I wouldn't go over that ground again."

I offer him the little bowl of mints and realize that I'm nervous. I hate the tremor in my fingers. I put the bowl down too quickly, and it makes a little bump. I can't help thinking of it as an advantage he has now. We sit together on the sofa, and Tom gets the children to come in one by one to kiss him, and to be exactly as mannerly as we taught them to be. My father says their names—John; Ellie; Morgan—and it strikes me that it's as if he's performing, as if they ought to be touched by the fact that he hasn't forgotten them. Although it's going to be full dark soon, I send them out to play in the yard. John is the oldest, and I tell him to watch the other two. He herds them out, being the older brother with them, acting like the responsibility gives him a headache. For a while we hear their voices outside. The whole thing feels rehearsed, and it embarrasses me. I'm starting to think how I have to give him my news just to cut my losses.

I hate being this way, feeling this confusion of anger and regret. It's why I'd rather he keep to his life and let me keep to mine. When I got married—against his strenuous objections—I told him I didn't want anything from him at all, and aside from the loan so we could buy this house, I've kept to it. We paid the loan back in the first year. We live modestly, which is the way we want it; we have always stood on our own and paid our own way.

Tom comes back with two martinis, and they start talking about Europe. Daddy goes on about the charms and pleasures of Rome. He thinks he may want to live there again. During the last ten years or so he's divided his time between Key West and the big sprawling ranch-style house he and what's her name, the actress he was married to for a while, built in the hills above Santa Monica. But now he says he's a little tired of the States. California bores him. Key West is all tourists these days. He might sell the houses and set himself up in Rome again.

"Rome," says Tom, who has never seen it. "Be fun to live in Rome, I guess."

"Rome's a long way from movieland," I say. "Aren't you going to make any more movies?"

My father shrugs.

"I always wanted to see Venice," Tom says.

"You said that once," my father tells him. "I remember."

Tom looks down into his drink, embarrassed. A kind, gentle man who happens never to have been overseas.

I WAS born in Rome. I don't remember much about living there, though we stayed until I was almost seven, when my father moved us all to New York. But he took James and me back to Italy during the summer of 1957, when James was sixteen and I was twelve. We stayed two months. He was unhappy about something, on a short fuse the whole time. I was in awe of him, of course, and though I didn't know the word, I thought he was omniscient. Certainly he knew how to read my mind. All I wanted to do was please him, and yet it seemed that everything I said caused him irritation and worry.

The woman he paid to watch us while he was off at the theater was German, and frightening. She wore an eye patch, and when he was gone she sometimes took it off to scare me. She always pretended to have forgotten it, but there was a gleam in her one eye. Her name was Brigitte (pronounced Brig-git-ee), and she'd been in the bombing of Berlin. She told me about it all, how she'd come from a rich Bavarian family, an old name, the name of a chain of German banks, though they were all either dead or poor now and the banks were owned by Western corporations. She was very bitter about the West. My father liked her efficiency, the fact that she kept everything so clean and took no guff, as he put it, from the younger citizens (his pet name for us). She took no guff from me. James was a different story altogether. James made her miserable, mostly by pretending not to notice her and by seeming to mistake her meaning all the time: he was always innocent, and his disobedience was always a mistake. And then of course he'd apologize in that empty way, when the apology is a weapon. "I know what you're doing, don't think I don't," Brigitte would say to him.

"What?" James would say, with his persecuted look. "What did I do? I thought you said we could go out after dinner."

"I said no, you could not go out."

"I didn't hear you right, then. Really. I was sure you said 'Go out.' That's what *I* heard, anyway. 'Go out.' I'm really sorry."

"You did it on purpose," I would say to him, desperate to keep him close. It only made him more determined to get away. About me, he couldn't have been less concerned: I was an irritation to him, a sloppy, crying kid always fighting him, always conniving to keep him from his escapes out into the frantic streets of Rome.

"The little girl says you knew you were disobeying me," Brigitte would say.

And James would answer her. "Oh, you going to believe a child over me?"

"I believe you wish to deceive me," said Brigitte, her face frowning into the black eye patch.

My father would come home to this frazzled, barely sane crank and listen to her reports on us: the little girl is too timid all the time and won't think for herself; the boy is devious and dishonest. "You need to spend more time at home, sir," said Brigitte, gathering her things and refusing to look at any of us, bustling out the door like someone whose mind is made up and will not return.

But she was always back in the morning, ready for more.

One evening I walked into the living room of that apartment on the Via Venetia and found my father grappling with her. She was bent over the back of the sofa, and he was holding her there, one hand tight along the side of her jaw. Her eye patch was on, and I couldn't see much else of her face. "Marilyn," my father said, stepping back. "What're you doing out of bed?"

I said nothing.

"Go back to bed," he told me, standing there while she straightened herself, pulling her dress down and brushing it against her thighs as if to wipe dust away.

"Do you hear me, kid? Go on to bed."

I did what he told me, and lay awake in that high-ceilinged room, so far from everything I knew, beginning to experience the eerie feeling that unlike other children I lived in a world where nothing was forbidden, where all impulses were equal, and equally possible to follow. I lay awake trembling, feeling the dark like something palpable, and when I went to sleep, finally, I dreamed of him and that woman in aspects of a kind of weird domesticity, not quite understanding any of it. When I woke the next morning, without knowing how or why, I understood that Brigitte would not be our baby-sitter anymore.

But I was wrong.

The following morning, she was there, twice as frightening as before and with a new confidence as if she were winning some game between us, drawing my father away. There were nights during that period, long nights with James gone on one of his forays into whatever trouble he could find, when everything she said and did convinced me that she would lure my father into something like a renunciation of me, as I knew he had renounced my dead mother. She seemed certain of it, certain of her place in the scheme of things. And of course she was wrong. A few days before we left, my father started bringing the actress home with him; the actress started sleeping over. And Brigitte became again the vaguely censorious, bustling figure going out the door in the evenings.

That was in Rome, the awful summer of 1957.

My father went back twice more and lived there again in the mid-sixties. By then he was married to the actress and I was in college, trying to keep people from guessing that I happened to be his daughter.

"So what's *1951* about?" Tom asks him now.

"The McCarthy hearings. The destruction of a man. Marilyn, do you remember David Shaw?"

"A political play," Tom says.

"Not exactly."

"You know what I remember about the McCarthy hearings?" I say. "Those awful pictures of the holocaust on television."

They both look at me.

"The hearings were on television at about the same time as that Walter Cronkite thing that showed all the pictures of the death camps," I tell them.

"Do you remember David Shaw?" my father says to me.

I tell him no.

"He played guitar. Sang country songs. He sat in our living room and played them. And you loved him. You don't remember him?"

I do in fact vaguely remember. "Yes," I say. "A little."

"The play's about him."

"I think those holocaust films were later," Tom says. "Weren't they?"

"No," I say. "I remember. I thought the two things were connected. The Army-McCarthy Hearings and those horrible pictures of the ovens."

"I don't recall what was on television," my father says. "But the play is about David Shaw."

"What about him?" I say.

"He was blacklisted," says my father.

Then Tom says, "You know, James turned up here recently."

I can't believe it. I can't believe he just blurted it out like that.

My father nods, not quite looking at either of us. "That so," he says.

"He's been staying with us," Tom says.

"How is he?"

Tom looks at me.

My father clears his throat and says, "I said, 'How is he?' "

"He's all right," I say. "I don't know what to tell you. Where to begin."

"He was on his way to Santa Monica," Tom says. "But then we told him you were in Rome."

"Is he thinking maybe he'd like to see me before I die?"

"He's been hurt," Tom says. "I mean, he's got a war wound, sort of."

"A *war* wound."

"Lebanon," I say. "He says he was doing something for the government."

"Jesus Christ," my father says.

"It's the left arm," Tom says. "It looks okay, but he can't move it."

"Where is he now?"

"In town," I say.

My father sits forward, puts his fingers to his nose, sniffs loud, looks at Tom. "I'd like another drink," he says.

Tom fixes it. While he's gone my father sits staring at the wall.

"I didn't know quite how to tell you," I say, and realize that it's the simple truth.

"Well—in fact I'd heard he was in the Middle East." When I stare at him, he shrugs. "I know a lot of people."

Tom comes back in with two more drinks. "Marilyn tell you about the job interviews?" he says. "James went to town for two interviews. He thinks he wants to live here in Point Royal."

My father drinks, swallows, seems to savor it. I look at his thick knuckles cradling the glass. These are not the hands of a man who works with books and papers; they look craggy and tough—the hands of a peasant farmer. He's extremely proud of this. He wears workshirts, flannels, denim overalls, wishing to accentuate the blocky, rustic look of his face and frame. Today he's wearing jeans and a gray turtleneck. His hair is drooping from the bare place in front, and he sweeps it across his brow with one muscular hand. It seems to me now that something about him has always frightened me, and perhaps it's this hayseed persona he likes to assume. I know what complexities lie under the homespun surface.

"So," he says. "James was headed for Santa Monica." It's as if he's merely trying to make conversation now.

"That's what he told us," I say.

He drinks, looking off. Across from us is a print Tom bought of houses in snow. I can guess what my father thinks of it, yet I feel like speaking up, saying something. I don't quite know what I'm supposed to feel now, but I don't want to let him see me worried about what his opinions are. I don't care what his opinions are. He's had four marriages, including the actress, and I don't even know who he's seeing these days. My mother was the first, and she died the year he left us. It was illness. There wasn't any connection. But I was six years old and I made a connection. As far as I'm concerned, his life is a series of public disasters.

"The prodigal returns," he says.

"What about David Shaw?" I say.

He shrugs.

Tom says, "The destruction of a man. Actually, I like that as a title."

"No. The title's *1951.*"

"What happened to David Shaw?" I say.

"Well, you'll have to see the play," he tells me.

When I was fourteen, he wrote a play in which my mother is portrayed as a character in the story of a writer's success— a small but tender contribution to the career. It was this play that set James against him for good—the whole country thinking of our mother as the dizzy but instinctively intelligent and sexually starved blond in *The Brace*. The big literary prize winner, and the actress he married won the Tony award playing this creation of his, this fantasy figure nothing like the real woman. James remembers her better than I do, and his rage is deeper than mine. I am mostly angry because I haven't had a normal life—because of his hatred of the life I've worked for here.

And he does hate it. He sits here on my sofa looking at the snow scenes on the wall and chewing the mints I've set before him, hating everything about the house, my husband and his job selling textbooks—our television and our fenced yard and the kids going to public school. The soap operas I used to watch whenever he was visiting, just to make his outrage complete. He doesn't even joke about it anymore: I'm a disappointment to him. I wonder sometimes if he sees my mother in me. In his play, she's not quite capable of a real thought without the help of the romantic figure who is remembering her in the first scene—the one where the sad, poetic figure stands over the grave and utters her name, utters the name of his sorrow, or words to that effect. But she provides the nourishment at the right time, and she senses something of his appetite for life, his rarity, his difference from her—his vividness and passion, his grave, all-consuming hunger for experience, his need. She senses these things, and something in her own limited emotional makeup mirrors them. Ironically, she dies before these possibilities in her soul can be released, but her simple-hearted, intuitive nurturing of the protagonist's aspirations proves instrumental. The artist learns that Love tends toward the particulars, the simple and the straightforward. Complexity is evil. Blah blah blah.

They teach this play in the colleges now. And my mother isn't immortalized in it, she's plagiarized. She doesn't even get to say her own lines.

"More to drink?" Tom says, and it dawns on me that we're all waiting for James to come back from town.

"I'd love some," my father says.

Tom brings the gin and vermouth and the ice bucket and sets it all on the coffee table before them. Now they sit next to each other, and I move to the chair across the room.

"So tell me about James," my father says, drinking.

"There are things *he* should tell you," I say.

"I want to know what I can before I see him." He doesn't even seem upset or nervous. He has always managed, even for his timidness about the matters of daily life, to glide through things as if trouble were habitat, the air he breathed.

"All right," I say. "There was a wife. They broke up. James spent some time in a hospital for nerves because of it."

"Breakdown?" he says.

"He just said he spent some time in a hospital," I say.

"So I've had a daughter-in-law I've never seen."

"And you've had wives *he's* never seen."

"Marilyn," Tom says, "don't do that."

They drink.

"Does he have any kids?" my father wants to know.

"None," I say.

"Jesus Christ," he says. "James. Well, I just can't believe it." He gulps the martini. Soon the world will start looking the way he likes it to look. "I was drunk almost the whole time I was in Europe."

"Are you bragging?" I say. I don't mean the sourness in my voice. I can't help it.

"Marilyn," Tom says.

"I drank the national drink of every country," says my father. "And I tried a thousand different wines and liqueurs. On one street in Naples I sat against the wall of a church like those wounded soldiers in Hemingway, and I got hauled away by the police."

"I never remember much of Hemingway," Tom says.

"Maybe it wasn't a church in Hemingway," my father says. "Anyway, that was the night I ran into Mark Loomis."

"Mark Loomis," I say. I have the same vague memory of him, around the time of David Shaw. I repeat the name.

"Mark Loomis," says my father. "Right. We worked together for a few years—Loomis and David Shaw and me. We were good friends. Loomis and I watched David Shaw get it but good in nineteen fifty-one. It was tremendously easy."

"That was a bad time, I guess," Tom says. He's feeling the martinis. And when he's feeling his drinks he's likely to be sincere enough about such a statement. Now he pours more gin into both glasses. It's not even seven o'clock in the evening.

JAMES went into town for two job interviews—one teaching high school, another managing a trade magazine. Both interviews were in the afternoon, so I know he's stopped off somewhere, is sitting in a bar watching the television and getting himself fortified for the night. I know this because James is fortifying himself every night these days.

Tom got the interviews for him because Tom knows a lot of teachers at the college and quite a few people in the trade publications business around the area. People trust him. And James, for all his talk those years ago about how I was throwing myself away on a man like Tom, is learning to appreciate someone who can get along in the practical world. What James has never had it in him to see, what my father never saw, is the way Tom is with the children, the delight he takes in them, the patience he shows each of them, and the love. They adore him. They don't care a bit if he never writes a book or delivers a reel of spy tape in the desert. They want somebody to be interested in their lives and to have time for them. Which is and has always been what I happen to want, too.

The conversation about the blacklisting is going on. "You can't be too careful, even these days," Tom says. "The mistake is thinking it won't happen because this is America."

"Quite perceptive," my father says, drinking. "That's the mistake a lot of them made. But I think it *is* a matter of not being foolhardy, too. I mean, that kind of faith is foolhardy.

Look at those poor students in China—that sad naive faith that the soldiers wouldn't kill them in cold blood."

"Foolhardy," Tom says. "Right."

"I'm going outside," I say.

"But now—listen," says my father, beginning to slur the words a little. "It's simply true there are personal reasons for what people do. Marilyn's mother, for instance. You know, she belonged to this—this club that got David Shaw in such trouble. She belonged to that club, too. Well, the poor woman grew up in Richmond—and *her* mother used to dress her up and invite the cream of polite society over for dinner. Every available young man with money and position, along with his parents. Used to send these people printed invitations, hundreds of printed invitations to get the four or five idiots who had nothing better to do than show up. And then, just as dinner was served, she'd leave Marilyn's mother there alone with them. Marilyn's mother ran away from that, finally. Went to New York on the train and got a job in a bank. That's where I met her. By that time she was a charter member of the club that David Shaw belonged to. You know what I'm talking about."

"I'm getting drunk," Tom says.

"You see—personal reasons—" my father waves one hand, vaguely, as if at an audience across the room. "You saw *The Brace*, didn't you? Lot of that's straight from life, see. Personal reasons. And—and people change. People are not the same. Very unpredictable."

These are the words of the famous playwright.

"I guess so," Tom tells him.

"So," my father says. "James has turned up."

"That's the crux of it," says Tom.

They're both getting tight.

"What was James doing in Lebanon?"

"He said something for the government."

"Never worked for a government in my life."

I get up and walk through the dining room to the kitchen and the dinner dishes. It's almost dark, and I can hear the children playing hide-and-seek in the yard. Something frantic in their voices makes me feel oddly as if all the energy is about to drain out of me. The world is all noise and confusion for a moment. Everything seems very precarious and dark. I turn the porch light on, and one of the kids, Ellie I think, yells for me to turn it off. I do. I stand in the light of the kitchen, gazing out at what I can see of the yard.

James walks out of the dark and up onto the first step.

"Hey," he says.

"Hey," I say.

He's holding the bad arm as if it hurts. Over the past few days, I've begun to realize it's a habit, like a tic. There's no feeling in the arm. "That's who I think it is, isn't it," he says, leaning up to look beyond me. "In there."

"James," I say.

"I guess I'm not ready to face him yet."

"James," I say, "what did you come here for?"

"You remember David Shaw?" he says.

I can't say anything for a second. The whole thing is like one of those absurd dreams unfolding until it begins to get scary. He smiles at me and in the bad light his face is both ghostly and like our mother's. "Sure you do," he says.

"What about him?" I say. "James, come in here now."

He steps back down into the grass. "I've got something important on Shaw. A diary. And the old man wants it."

Again I can't say anything.

"I'm going to go have some more fortification for this," he says. "More than I originally thought. I'm just not ready yet. I can't stand him unless I'm completely crocked. Is he drunk yet?"

"James," I say. "For God's sake."

But he's already off in the dark, a moving shadow going across the lawns like a prowler. He's going on, and I hear my oldest, John, take a pretend potshot at him. "You got me, sport," James says, low. Then he's gone.

When I turn back into the kitchen, my father's standing at the counter with the ice bucket and the bottles. "Condensation on your coffee table," he says. "I'm making the drinks out here."

I watch him.

"I should've mentioned that I saw James in Italy," he says. "Sorry. It wasn't a very fruitful conversation. I did manage to get some information from him about something I was looking for. I guess I told him I was going back to Santa Monica. But I stayed in Rome awhile."

"You let us go on like that."

"Well," he says. "It was months ago."

I feel suddenly cheated somehow, yet I can't put my finger on it. There's something wrong with the two of them meeting in Italy while I'm here, going on in the assumption that they're estranged. I can't explain it. But it drops into me like something going down a deep well, and for a minute I can't do anything but stand there and breathe.

"Do you want a drink?" he says.

"No," I tell him.

"That was James out there, wasn't it?"

I nod.

"He coming in?"

"He went to fortify himself."

"A phrase he got from me."

I say nothing. He's got both drinks now, and he turns slightly to look at me.

"Loomis—that I ran into in Rome. He was in touch with James. There's some stuff about David Shaw—"

I interrupt him. "James told me."

"It's just something Shaw gave him. And he'd left at home. James was older, remember. Shaw made it a game between the two of them, you know, like pretending to be spies."

"Yes," I say.

My father shakes his head. "Shaw was all glittery courage. But he was crazy at the end."

"I remember him," I say.

"Well." He turns. Then he stops, looks back at me. "My whole life I never had an ounce of the kind of integrity he had. Him or your mother. You know, and it's always hurt me to know it. All I do—all I ever did—is make little costume dramas—it's all I'm good for. And I was unwilling to take even the smallest risk that I'd ever be stopped from doing it. The one thing I do well—"

"Oh, look," I say.

"Right," he says. "For a second there I forgot who I was talking to."

"I am not beneath you," I tell him.

He says nothing for a moment.

"I have done what I wanted to do," I say. "Exactly the same as you."

"I was confessing something to you," he says.

"Your confessions are too easy. You're too glib about them."

"After all," he says. "I deal in words."

"You make lies," I say.

"I know this," he answers. "You're talking about *The Brace*. Would it interest you to know that your mother wanted me out of the house when I left?"

"And that's why you portrayed her like that?"

"Well," he says. "I should know by now I can't argue this with you or James, either. I can't help the material, though. There's almost nothing of intention in it. There's not the remotest wish to bruise, either."

Tom walks in. He's heard the tones in our voices, and he's pitched himself into the middle of us, wanting to make harmony and friendship. He kisses the side of my face and, moving a little unsteadily to the refrigerator, opens it. "Never mind that drink," he says to my father. "I'm just going to have a beer."

My father drinks Tom's martini down and sets the glass on the counter. He holds the other glass up to me as if to offer a toast. "Cheers," he says. "And God bless our differences, too." Then he turns and walks out of the room.

Tom opens his beer and leans against the counter, looking at me.

"What?" I say.

"Just hoping for a little peace," he says.

"You've got it," I say, heading out. But he takes me by the arm.

"Wait, honey."

"Tom," my father calls from the other room.

"Peace?" Tom says to me.

I look at him, and because he wants to, he reads acceptance in my face. They don't even like you, I want to tell him. But I hold it back.

"Come join us," he says, turning from me. I watch him go down the hall, and then I move to the back door, half expecting to see James out on the porch. But there's only the vast dark, and the thrown light of the doorway on the lawn, with my shadow in it. I step outside, close the door quietly. On the side patio, in the dark, I find my oldest, John, sitting alone in the portable hammock, struggling with the apparently loose hinges of a pair of scissors. In a little bare place in the trees beyond the end of the lawn, Ellie and Morgan are trying to jump rope. Ellie's only five and can't do it. Morgan, who's seven, can. They're arguing about the difference. John, just last week, celebrated his thirteenth birthday by cutting the skin above his anklebone with a paring knife he'd stolen from the kitchen. He'd been playing mumblety-peg with it. Someone at school had taught him the game, apparently.

"What're you doing?" I ask.

He's startled but quickly recovers, smiling at me, conning me. "I found these," he says. Lately I can't control him; I think of James with Brigitte in a place like Rome—so far away, and like a minute ago: the easy lies, the deceptions through half-truths, the feigned confusion. For a little space, like a heartbeat, I feel so very tired of everything, and the idea of holding onto some kind of love seems almost idiotic. In another time I'll stand before my grown son with my own complications, and he will have his. Everything will have worn down between us. It's hard to believe anything matters much, and I can hear my father's voice in the other room, holding forth. He's lecturing Tom now, and Tom—because he's had too much to drink—is interested. It's the old pattern of the first night when my father makes one of his stops. Tomorrow they'll both be hung over, and they'll tease about it, as if they've accomplished something, traveled through something risky and wonderful.

I reach down and take the scissors from John. "Come on," I say. "Time for a bath."

"A bath," he says. "It's early. It's not all the way dark yet."

"Come on, honey," I say, nearly crying. "Please don't argue with me about it."

He gets up, starts out to collect the other two. Their contending voices come from the shadows in the yard; they're only shapes now. Beyond them the moon is bright. I go and stand in the doorway and wait for them, and I can hear Tom laughing in the other room.

In a little while James will come home. He'll have had a few; he'll have fortified himself. He'll come in and find his father sitting with Tom, and they'll all be drunk no matter what else they are. It'll be what you'd expect. Tom will mediate, will be friendly and concerned—they'll be polite for his benefit, these men who don't have any idea of his qualities, his tenderness and grace, his humor; his dear old, simple wish to be pleasant. His wonder about his own children, and his life that he attends to after he attends to theirs. Probably nothing much will get said that anyone remembers. My father will go home and write a play about a man he betrayed, and the play will be full of powerful remorse. It will be exactly what he truly feels but has never been able to express with people, just talking, saying things out. James will no doubt continue with his journey back to something— and perhaps he'll travel to California soon. Tom will go to work, vaguely mad at himself for allowing them to look down on him but already forgetting the whole thing, already forgiving it. It is his nature to forgive, as it is mine to remember.

But tonight, in the haze of what they have had to drink, they'll find all sorts of things to say and laugh at and offer an opinion on, and they'll be loud and sentimental and brotherly with each other. This is what is ahead, I think. I can see it clearly, as if it has already happened. My father, my brother and my husband. And I come to know, with a sense of discouragement like a swoon, that at a certain point in the night, while I lie in bed remembering myself at twelve years old—a little girl on a wide bed in an apartment in Rome, with a strange woman in the next room and no one to lean on, nothing at all to brace her—I'll hear their voices on the other side of the wall, and I won't be able to distinguish which of them is which.

THE EYES
OF LOVE

THIS particular Sunday in the third year of their marriage, the Truebloods are leaving a gathering of the two families—a cookout at Kenneth's parents' that has lasted well into the night and ended with his father telling funny stories about being in the army in Italy just after the war. The evening has turned out to be exactly the kind of raucous, beery gathering Shannon said it would be, trying to beg off going. She's pregnant, faintly nauseous all the time, and she's never liked all the talk. She's heard the old man's stories too many times.

"They're good stories," Kenneth said that morning as she poured coffee for them both.

"I've heard every one of them at least twice," said Shannon. "God knows how many times your mother has heard them."

He said, "You might've noticed everybody laughing when he tells them, Shannon. Your father laughs until I start thinking about his heart."

"He just wants to be a part of the group."

"He chokes on it," Kenneth said, feeling defensive and oddly embarrassed, as if some unflattering element of his personality had been cruelly exposed. "Jesus, Shannon. Sometimes I wonder what goes through your mind."

"I just don't feel like listening to it all," she told him. "Does it have to be a statement of some kind if I don't go? Can't you just say I'm tired?"

"Your father and sisters are supposed to be there."

"Well, I'm pregnant—can't I be tired?"

"What do you think?" Kenneth asked her, and she shook

her head, looking discouraged and caught. "It's just a cook-out," he went on. "Cheer up—maybe no one will want to talk."

"That isn't what I mean, and you know it," she said.

Now she rolls the window down on her side and waves at everybody. "See you," she calls as Kenneth starts the car. For a moment they are sitting in the roar and rattle of the engine, which backfires and sends up a smell of burning oil and exhaust. Everyone's joking and calling to them, and Kenneth's three brothers begin teasing about the battered Ford Kenneth lacks the money to have fixed. As always he feels a suspicion that their jokes are too much at his expense, home from college four years and still out of a job in his chosen field, there being no college teaching jobs to be had anywhere in the region. He makes an effort to ignore his own misgiving, and anyway most of what they say is obliterated by the noise. He races the engine, and everyone laughs. It's all part of the uproar of the end of the evening, and there's good feeling all around. The lawn is illuminated with floodlights from the top of the house, and Kenneth's father stands at the edge of the sidewalk with one arm over *her* father's broad shoulders. Both men are a little tight.

"Godspeed," Kenneth's father says, with a heroic wave.

"Good-bye," says Shannon's father.

The two men turn and start unsteadily back to the house, and the others, Kenneth's mother and brothers and Shannon's two younger sisters, are applauding and laughing at the dizzy progress they make along the walk. Kenneth backs out of the driveway, waves at them all again, honks the horn and pulls away.

Almost immediately his wife gives forth a conspicuous expression of relief, sighing deeply and sinking down in the seat. This makes him clench his jaw, but he keeps silent.

The street winds among trees in the bright fan of his head-lights; it's going to be a quiet ride home. He's in no mood to talk now. She murmurs something beside him in the dark, but he chooses to ignore it. He tries to concentrate on driving, staring out at the road as if alone. After a little while she puts the radio on, looks for a suitable station, and the noise begins to irritate him, but he says nothing. Finally she gives up, turns the radio off. The windshield is dotting with rain. They come to the end of the tree-lined residential street, and he pulls out toward the city. Here the road already shimmers with water, the reflected lights of shops and buildings going on into the closing perspective of brightnesses ahead.

"Are you okay to drive?" she asks.

"What?" he says, putting the wipers on.

"I just wondered. You had a few beers."

"I had three beers."

"You had a few."

"Three," he says. "And I didn't finish the last one. What're you doing, counting them now?"

"Somebody better count them."

"I had three goddamn beers," he says.

In fact, he hadn't finished the third beer because he'd begun to experience heartburn shortly after his father started telling the stories. He's sober all right, full of club soda and coffee, and he feels strangely lucid, as if the chilly night with its rain-smelling breezes has brought him wider awake, some-how. He puts both hands on the wheel and hunches forward slightly, meaning to ignore her shape, so quiet beside him. He keeps right at the speed limit, heading into the increasing rain, thinking almost abstractly about her.

"What're you brooding about?" she says.

The question surprises him. "I don't know," he says. "I'm driving."

"You're mad at me."

"No."

"Sure?" she asks.

"I'm sure."

WHAT he is sure of is that the day has been mostly ruined for him: the entire afternoon and evening spent in a state of vague tension, worrying about his wife's mood, wondering about what she might say or do or refuse to do in light of that mood. And the vexing thing is that toward the end, as he watched her watch his father tell the stories, the sense of something guilty began to stir in his soul, as if this were all something he had betrayed her into having to endure and there was something lurid or corrupt about it—an immoral waste of energy somehow, like a sort of spiritual gluttony. He's trying hard not to brood about it, but he keeps seeing her in the various little scenes played out during the course of the day—her watchfulness during his own clowning with his brothers and her quiet through the daylong chatter of simple observation and remarking that had gone on with her father and sisters, with Kenneth's parents. In each scene she seemed barely able to contain her weariness and boredom.

At one point while his father was basking in the laughter following a story about wine and a small boy in Rome who knew where the Germans had stored untold gallons of it, Kenneth stared at Shannon until she saw him, and when for his benefit she seemed discreetly to raise one eyebrow (it was just between them), her face, as she looked back at his father, took on a glow of tolerance along with the weariness it had worn—and something like affectionate exasperation, too.

Clearly she meant it as a gift to him, for when she looked at him again she smiled.

He might've smiled back. He had been laughing at something his father said. Again, though, he thought he saw the faintest elevation of one of her eyebrows.

This expression, and the slight nod of her head, reminded

him with a discomforting nostalgic stab (had they come so far from there?) of the look she had given him from the other side of noisy, smoky rooms in rented campus houses, when they were in graduate school and had first become lovers and moved with a crowd of radical believers and artists, people who were somehow most happy when they were wakeful and ruffled in the drugged hours before dawn—after the endless far-flung hazy discussions, the passionate sophomoric talk of philosophy and truth and everything that was wrong with the world and the beautiful changes everyone expected.

Someone would be talking, and Shannon would somehow confide in him with a glance from the other side of the room. There had been a thrill in receiving this look from her, since it put the two of them in cahoots; it made them secret allies in a kind of dismissal, a superiority reserved for the gorgeous and the wise. And this time he thought for a moment that she was intending the look, intending for him to think about those other days, before the job market had forced them to this city and part-time work for his father; before the worry over rent and the pregnancy had made everything of their early love seem quite dreamy and childish. He almost walked over to take her hand. But then a moment later she yawned deeply, making no effort to conceal her sleepiness, and he caught himself wishing that for the whole of the evening he could have managed not to look her way at all. With this thought in his mind, he did walk over to her. "I guess you want to go."

"For two hours," she said.

"You should've told me."

"I think I did."

"No," he said.

"I'm too tired to think," she told him.

* * *

Now, driving through the rainy night, he glances over at her and sees that she's simply staring out the passenger window, her hands open in her lap. He wants to be fair. He reminds himself that she's never been the sort of person who feels comfortable—or with whom one feels comfortable—at a party: something takes hold of her; she becomes objective and heavily intellectual, sees everyone as species, somehow, everything as behavior. A room full of people laughing and having a good innocent time is nevertheless a manifestation of some kind of pecking order to her: such a gathering means nothing more than a series of meaningful body languages and gestures, nothing more than the forms of competition, and, as she has told him on more than one occasion, she refuses to allow herself to be drawn in; she will not play social games. He remembers now that in their college days he considered this attitude of hers to be an element of her sharp intelligence, her wit. He had once considered that the two of them were above the winds of fashion, intellectual and otherwise; he had once been proud of this quirk of hers.

It's all more complicated than that now, of course. Now he knows she's unable to help the fear of being with people in congregation, that it's all a function of her having been refused affection when she was a child, of having been encouraged to compete with her many brothers and sisters for the attentions of her mother, who over the years has been in and out of mental institutions, and two of whose children, Shannon's older sisters, grew sexually confused in their teens and later underwent sex-change operations. They are now two older brothers. Shannon and Kenneth have made jokes about this, but the truth is, she comes from a tremendously unhappy family. The fact that she's managed to put a marriage together is no small accomplishment. She's fought to overcome the confusion and troubles of her life at home, and she's mostly succeeded. When her father finally divorced her mother, Shannon was the one he came to for support; it was Shannon who helped get him situated with the two younger sisters; and it was Shannon who forgave him all the excesses he had been driven to by the mad excesses of her mother. Shannon doesn't like to talk about what she remembers of growing up, but Kenneth often thinks of her as a little girl in a house where nothing is what it ought to be. He would say she has a right to her temperament, her occasional paranoia in groups of people—and yet for some time now, in spite of all efforts not to, he's felt only exasperation and annoyance with her about it.

As he has felt annoyance about several other matters: her late unwillingness to entertain; her lack of energy; and her reluctance to have sex. She has only begun to show slightly, yet she claims she feels heavy and unsexy. He understands this, of course, but it worries him that when they're sitting together quietly in front of the television set and she reaches over and takes his hand—a simple gesture of affection from a woman expecting a child—he finds himself feeling itchy and irritable, aware of the caress as a kind of abbreviation, an abridgement: she doesn't mean it as a prelude to anything. He wants to be loving and gentle through it all, and yet he can't get rid of the feeling that this state of affairs is what she secretly prefers.

WHEN she moves on the front seat next to him, her proximity actually startles him.

"What?" she says.

"I didn't say anything."

"You jumped a little."

"No," he says.

"All right." She settles down in the seat again.

A moment later he looks over at her. He wants to have

the sense of recognition and comfort he has so often had when gazing upon her. But her face looks faintly deranged in the bad light, and he sees that she's frowning, pulling something down into herself. Before he can suppress it, anger rises like a kind of heat in the bones of his face. "Okay, what is it?" he says.

"I wish I was in bed."

"You *didn't* say anything to me about going," he says.

"Would you have listened?"

"I would've listened, sure," he says. "What kind of thing to say is that?"

She's silent, staring out her window.

"Look," he says, "just exactly what is it that's bothering you?"

She doesn't answer right away. "I'm tired," she tells him without quite turning to look at him.

"No, really," he says. "I want to hear it. Come on, let it out."

Now she does turn. "I told you this morning. I just don't like hearing the same stories all the time."

"They aren't all the same," he says, feeling unreasonably angry.

"Oh, of course they are. God—you were asking for them. Your mother deserves a medal."

"I like them. Mom likes them. Everybody likes them. Your father and your sisters like them."

"Over and over," she mutters, looking away again. "I just want to go to sleep."

"You know what your problem is?" he says. "You're a *critic*. That's what your problem is. Everything is something for you to evaluate and *decide* on. Even me. Especially me."

"You," she says.

"Yes," he says. "Me. Because this isn't about my father at all. It's about us."

She sits staring at him. She's waiting for him to go on. On an impulse, wanting to surprise and upset her, he pulls the car into a 7-Eleven parking lot and stops.

"What're you doing?" she says.

He doesn't answer. He turns the engine off and gets out, walks through what he is surprised to find is a blowing storm across to the entrance of the store and in. It's noisy here—five teenagers are standing around a video game while another is rattling buttons and cursing. Behind the counter an old man sits reading a magazine and sipping from a steaming cup. He smiles as Kenneth approaches, and for some reason Kenneth thinks of Shannon's father, with his meaty red hands and unshaven face, his high-combed double crown of hair and missing front teeth. Shannon's father looks like the Ukrainian peasant farmer he's descended from on the un-Irish side of that family. He's a stout, dull man who simply watches and listens. He has none of the sharp expressiveness of his daughter, yet it seems to Kenneth that he is more friendly—even, somehow, more tolerant. Thinking of his wife's boredom as a kind of aggression, he buys a pack of cigarettes, though he and Shannon quit smoking more than a year ago. He returns to the car, gets in without looking at her, dries his hands on his shirt, and tears at the cigarette pack.

"Oh," she says. "Okay—great."

He pulls out a cigarette and lights it with the dashboard lighter. She's sitting with her arms folded, still hunched down in the seat. He blows smoke. He wants to tell her, wants to set her straight somehow; but he can't organize the words in his mind yet. He's too angry. He wants to smoke the cigarette and then measure everything out for her, the truth as it seems to be arriving in his heart this night: that she's manipulative and mean when she wants to be, that she's devious and self-absorbed and cruel of spirit when she doesn't get her way—looking at his father like that, as if there were something sad about being able to hold a room in thrall at the age of seventy-five. Her own father howling with laughter the whole time . . .

"When you're through with your little game, I'd like to go home," she says.

"Want a cigarette?" he asks.

"This is so childish, Kenneth."

"Oh?" he says. "How childish is it to sit and *sulk* through an entire party because people don't conform to your wishes and—well, Jesus, I'm sorry, I don't think I quite know what the hell you wanted from everybody today. Maybe you could fill me in on it a little."

"I want some understanding from you," she says, beginning to cry.

"Oh, no," says Kenneth. "You might as well cut that out. I'm not buying that. Not the way you sat yawning at my father tonight as if he was senile or something and you couldn't even be bothered to humor him."

"*Humor* him. Is that what everyone's doing?"

"You know better than that, Shannon. Either that or you're blind."

"All right," she says. "That was unkind. Now I don't feel like talking anymore, so let's just drop it."

He's quiet a moment, but the anger is still working in him. "You know the trouble with you?" he says. "You don't see anything with love. You only see it with your *brain*."

"Whatever you say," she tells him.

"Everything's locked up in your *head*," he says, taking a long drag of the cigarette and then putting it out in the ashtray. He's surprised by how good he feels—how much in charge, armed with being right about her: he feels he's made a discovery, and he wants to hold it up into the light and let her look at it.

"God, Kenneth. I felt sick all day. I'm pregnant."

He starts the car. "You know those people that live behind us?" he says. The moment has become almost philosophical to him.

She stares at him with her wet eyes, and just now he feels quite powerful and happy.

"Do you?" he demands.

"Of course I do."

"Well, I was watching them the other day. The way he is with the yard—right? We've been making such fun of him all summer. We've been so *smart* about his obsession with weeds and trimming and the almighty grass."

"I guess it's really important that we talk about these people now," she says. "Jesus."

"I'm telling you something you need to hear," Kenneth says. "Goddammit."

"I don't want to hear it now," she says. "I've been listening to talk all day. I'm tired of talk."

And Kenneth is shouting at her. "I'll just say this and then I'll shut up for the rest of the goddamn year if that's what you want!"

She says nothing.

"I'm telling you about these people. The man was walking around with a little plastic baggie on one hand, picking up the dog's droppings. Okay? And his wife was trimming one of the shrubs. She was trimming one of the shrubs and I thought for a second I could feel what she was thinking. There wasn't anything in her face, but I was so *smart*, like we are, you know, Shannon. I was so smart about it that I knew what she was thinking. I was so *perceptive* about these people we don't even know. These people we're too snobbish to speak to."

"You're the one who makes fun of them," Shannon says.

"Let me finish," he says. "I saw the guy's wife look at him

from the other side of the yard, and it was like I could hear the words in her mind: 'My God, he's picking up the dog droppings again. I can't stand it another minute.' You know? But that *wasn't* what she was thinking. Because she walked over in a little while and helped him—actually pointed out a couple of places he'd missed, for God's sake. And then the two of them walked into their house arm in arm with their dog droppings. You see what I'm saying, Shannon? That woman was looking at him with love. She didn't see what I saw—there wasn't any criticism in it."

"I'm not criticizing anyone," his wife tells him. "I'm tired. I need to go home and get some sleep."

"But you *were* criticizing," he says, pulling back out into traffic. "Everything you did was a criticism. Don't you think it shows? You didn't even try to stifle any of it."

"Who's doing the criticizing now?" she says. "Are you the only one who gets to be a critic?"

He turns down the city street that leads home. He's looking at the lights going off in the shining, rainy distances. Beside him, his pregnant wife sits crying. There's not much traffic, but he seems to be traveling at just the speed to arrive at each intersection when the light turns red. At one light they sit for what seems an unusually long time, and she sniffles. And quite abruptly he feels wrong; he thinks of her in the bad days of her growing up and feels sorry for her. "Okay," he says. "Look, I'm sorry."

"Just let's be quiet," she says. "Can we just be quiet? God, if I could just not have the sound of *talk* for a while."

The car idles roughly, and the light doesn't change. He looks at the green one two blocks away and discovers in himself the feeling that some momentous outcome hinges on that light staying green long enough for him to get through it. With a weird pressure behind his eyes, everything shifts toward some inner region of rage and chance and fright: it's as if his whole life, his happiness, depends on getting through that signal before it, too, turns red. He taps his palm on the steering wheel, guns the engine a little like a man at the starting line of a race.

"Honey," she says. "I didn't mean to hurt your feelings."

He doesn't answer. His own light turns green, and in the next instant he's got the pedal all the way to the floor. They go roaring through the intersection, the tires squealing, the back of the car fishtailing slightly in the wetness. She's at his side, quiet, bracing in the seat, her hands out on the dash, and in the moment of knowing how badly afraid she is he feels strangely reconciled to her, at a kind of peace, speeding through the rain. He almost wishes something would happen, something final, watching the light ahead change to yellow, then to red. It's close, but he makes it through. He makes it through and then realizes she's crying, staring out, the tears streaming down her face. He slows the car, wondering at himself, holding on to the wheel with both hands, and at the next red light he comes to a slow stop. When he sees that her hands are now resting on her abdomen, he thinks of her pregnancy as if for the first time; it goes through him like a bad shock to his nerves. "Christ," he says, feeling sick. "I'm sorry."

The rain beats at the windows and makes gray, moving shadows on the inside of the car. He glances at her, then looks back at the road.

"Honey?" she says. The broken note in her voice almost makes him wince.

He says, "Don't, it's all right." He's sitting there looking through the twin half-circles of water the wipers make.

She sniffles again.

"Shannon," he says. "I didn't mean any of it." But his own voice sounds false to him, a note higher, somehow, and it dawns on him that he's hoarse from shouting. He thinks of the weekend mornings they've lain in bed, happy and warm, luxuriating in each other. It feels like something in the distant past to him. And then he remembers being awakened by the roar of the neighbor's power mower, the feeling of superiority he had entertained about such a man, someone obsessed with a lawn. He's thinking of the man now, that one whose wife sees whatever she sees when she looks at him, and perhaps she looks at him with love.

Shannon is trying to gain control of herself, sobbing and coughing. The light changes, but no one's behind him, and so he moves over in the seat and puts his arms around her. A strand of her hair tickles his jaw, a little discomfort he's faintly aware of. He sits very still, saying nothing, while in the corner of his vision the light turns yellow, then red again. She's holding on to him, and she seems to nestle slightly. When the light turns back to green, she gently pulls away from him.

"We better go," she says, wiping her eyes.

He sits straight, presses the accelerator pedal carefully, like a much older man. He wishes he were someone else, wishes something would change, and then is filled with a shivering sense of the meaning of such thoughts. He's driving on in the rain, and they are silent for a time. They're almost home.

"I'm just so tired," Shannon says finally.

"It's all right," he tells her.

"Sweet," she says.

The fight's over. They've made up. She reaches across and gives his forearm a little affectionate squeeze. He takes her hand and squeezes back. Then he has both hands on the wheel again. Their apartment house is in sight now, down the street to the left. He turns to look at her, his wife, here in the shadowed and watery light, and then he quickly looks back at the road. It comes to him like a kind of fright that in the little idle moment of his gaze some part of him was marking the unpleasant downturn of her mouth, the chiseled, too-sharp curve of her jaw—the whole, disheveled, vaguely tattered look of her—as though he were a stranger, someone unable to imagine what anyone, another man, other men, someone like himself, could see in her to love.

LUCK

I CAME back in no time with the burgers, and when he reached into the bag I smelled it on him. I didn't say anything. He got his burger and opened it, talking goofy like he does. "Best car ever made was the Studebaker, Baker."

"Right, Dwight," I said, but my heart wasn't in it.

He sat on the stairs and I sat in the window seat of this place. We'd got the walls and the first coat of trim. There was a lot of touch-up to do, and if he was going to start drinking, it wasn't going to get done. Outside, we still had the porch railing. It was a big wraparound porch. Two days' work at least, with both of us pushing it.

"Dad," I said.

He was chewing, shaking his head. He liked the hamburger. All his life, I think he enjoyed things more than other people. "Man," he said.

It was getting dark. We still had to finish the trim in the dining room—the chair railing. "Well," I said. I was watching his eyes.

"You know," he said. "I do good work. Don't I do good work?"

"The finest," I said.

He smiled. "And you help me."

I concentrated on my food. I could've maybe figured I'd made a mistake until now. But this was the way he talked whenever he was on the stuff. I started looking around casually for where he could hide it.

"You're a good son," he said.

I might've nodded. I was eating that hamburger and trying not to show anything to him.

"Twenty years ago I painted my first house," he said. "Helped a friend one summer. I told you this. Never dreamed I'd have a son to help me. You ought to be in college, son. But I'm just as glad you're here."

It was like he might start crying.

"Best get back to work," I said.

He was sitting there thinking. I knew what he was seeing in his mind. "Your mother sure can pick them," he said. "I don't know what she saw in me."

I stood. I had what was left of my burger in my hand. I put it in the bag and went over to the paint can.

"Hey," he said.

I said, "Hey."

"I said I don't know what she saw in me."

"Me either," I said.

"Good thing you look like her," he said.

"Right, Dwight," I said.

"That's the truth, Ruth," he said. He was still sitting there.

"You want me to do the second coat in here?" I said.

"Naw. Get the dining room."

I said, "Okay."

"Hey," he said. "What if I take you and your mother out to dinner tonight?"

"That'd be all right," I told him.

"Okay," he said. "You're on."

"Great," I said. It was getting dark. We'd been eating burgers.

"You think she'll feel like going out?" he said.

"Got me," I said.

"She's been staying in the house too much. Working too hard. There's no need for her to put so much time in every day. Right?"

I said, "Sure."

"Yeah," he said. "And you've been working hard."

"Yes, sir," I said.

"You think we did a good job here so far?" He stood up and looked around at everything.

I did the same. I saw that over the kitchen cabinets, where he'd been painting when I left to get the burgers, it was going to need a lot of touching up. There were places he'd missed. He'd been hurrying it. You couldn't mistake a thing like that. Back before he was too bad, when I was small, he used to take me through the houses when he was finished with them, and he would point out where other painters cut corners and he didn't. He'd show me the places where he'd taken the extra step and done it right. He was teaching me. Do a thing, boy, you do it right the first time. You take pride in what you do. He drummed it into me. You go that extra mile. You take pains. People remember good work. People remember excellence. And when I worked with him summers and he was okay, he'd do a thing, put the last touch on something, and he'd stand back and look at it, proud as hell. "New money," he'd say.

And I'd say, "New money."

You could hear the satisfaction in the way he breathed, looking at what he'd done.

That was when he was okay.

"Little touch-up over the sink," he said to me now.

I didn't answer.

"Well. I better get off to the bank before they close the drive-in window."

"The bank," I said.

He didn't look at me. "The bank, Frank."

I just stared at him. For a long time we were like that, you know. Staring at each other from opposite sides of the room, with the tarpaulin and the paint cans between us like we were listening for some sound.

"How'm I going to take you guys out to eat without some money, honey?" he said.

"Oh," I said. "Right."

"You go ahead and finish what you can in the dining room."

I nodded.

"We straight?"

"Straight," I said.

It was what we always said when he'd had to discipline me, and he'd come in afterward and explain the punishment. We'd been saying it like a joke between us since I was sixteen.

"Sure?" he said.

"Very, Jerry," I said.

He put his hand out with the thumbs-up sign. "I'll be back, Jack."

"Okay," I said.

I watched him get out of his coveralls, because I thought it might fall out of one of the pockets. He laid them across the kitchen counter, then smoothed his hair back with both hands and looked at me. "Don't bust yourself," he said. "We did enough for one day."

"Right," I said.

I knew what would happen now. He went into the bathroom, and flushed the toilet. When he came out he went to the door and got himself through it quick, calling back to me that he'd be five minutes. I stood by the front window and watched him get into the truck. He wouldn't be back tonight. He wouldn't be back for days maybe. A week. Then we'd get the call. We'd go get him. He'd be in the hospital again, going through the treatment. This is all stuff you know. You don't need me to paint the picture.

I went back into the dining room. There was a lot of work to do. These people were supposed to occupy in two days, and it wasn't going to get finished now. No way. But I started on it just the same. I was sick, thinking of what tonight was going to be like. Everything she'd gone through over the years. And the thing was, there didn't seem to be anything in particular that triggered it. When she met him, she told me, he was a kid who liked a drink. She did, too. He'd get plowed and sometimes she'd get plowed with him. But they were always okay afterward and she couldn't say when it had happened that he didn't stop. She'll tell you now she doesn't know where it went over the line and the stuff got ahold of him. You have to know that he was never the kind that got mean or violent, either. That was the thing. You could walk away from somebody who knocked you around. The worst he ever did was disappear, and he did that often enough for me to know it was happening again. But when he started, it was always that he loved everybody. He'd cry and be sad and incredibly gentle. And when he was sober again he was always very sorry. Sometimes he was good for months at a time, and when he was, you couldn't find anybody better as a companion and a friend. You could trust him with your life.

Which was why I let him go like I did, knowing what he was up to. I didn't for the life of me have the heart not to trust him one more time.

Anyway, I was going to paint all night. I was going to get it done. I figured after a while, when we didn't show up, she'd come looking for us, and she'd know. She'd pull up and see the truck gone and all the lights burning. I didn't want to have to look at her when she knew again, but there wasn't anything for it.

I worked maybe an hour. I got into the work, into the rhythm of the whole task. We had the blaster there, but the tapes were all his: Beatles and the Stones. Aretha Franklin. It's something like rock 'n' roll, anyway. There's guitars and drums. It sounds enough like what I like, so I never complain. But I was just working in the quiet, and so I heard the truck pull in. I can't say what that did to me. He had gone to the bank, like he said. I mean, that's what I thought. I heard the engine quit, the door open and close. I worked on. I wanted him to find me working. Then I thought I'd give him something, and I got over to the blaster real fast and put the Beatles on. The Beatles were all over that house. Revolution. I was going at it in the dining room, moving myself to the music, and when I turned to smile at him I saw the guy who was having this place built, the owner. Big, heavy, bearded guy, looking like somebody with not much patience. I'd seen him walking around the lot when we first knew we were going to have the job and it was nothing more than a hole in the ground.

"Hey," I said.

He was standing in the doorway, looking at me. I went over and turned the music off. He'd walked on into the family room. "You do nice work," he said. He was looking at the mantel. There were several places I could see that needed a touch. "Is it dry?" he said.

"Not quite yet," I said.

"Listen," he said. "Are you going to finish in two days?" I nodded. I felt awful.

"You do work fast," he said. "I was in here yesterday and none of this was done yet."

"Yes, sir," I told him.

"Looks good," he said. He was moving around the room now, appreciating everything. It *was* good work. We had done real good work together for this part of it.

When we got to the living room, which was the most finished, I said, "My dad's the one who painted in here."

"He does nice work," the guy said. "Very nice."

"Yes," I said. "My dad always says—you know. Do a job with pride." If I started crying, I thought, I might hit him. I never felt that way before. If he noticed something wrong anywhere, I just wasn't sure what would happen.

"It shows," he said, smiling at me. "The pride shows."

"Yeah," I said.

"You must be very proud of your dad."

I looked at him. For a second I wasn't sure what he knew.

"What's it like, working with your father?"

"It's great," I said.

"Well," he turned and appreciated the room. "You don't find quality work these days. It's refreshing to find it."

"If you don't do a job right," I said. I just wanted him to get out of there before something happened. I was breathing hard. I had this awful tightness in my throat, like I was a kid and I'd got caught doing something wrong.

"These days," he said. "You give a kid an inch and he takes a mile, you know? Does your father trust you?"

"Sure," I said. I was watching the way his hands moved near his mouth. Something was on his nerves, and it made me nervous.

"You work like hell to give them something and a lot of them just throw it in your face. You know—drugs. Disobedience. Insolence, really. Hell, defiance. I think—working like this, with your father. I think that's a good thing. I wish I did something that my son could do with me, you know?"

I just nodded.

"You can't ask a kid to help you sell stocks in the summer. It's not a thing you can do together."

"No," I said.

"When I was your age, you know what I wanted to be? I wanted to be a carpenter. I sometimes wish I'd done it."

"Never too late," I told him.

"I wouldn't know." He was thinking hard about something, looking off. Then he said, "I guess you communicate pretty well."

I didn't know what he meant.

"You and your father."

"Oh," I said. "Yeah." I couldn't look at him.

"Must—must be nice."

"It's okay," I said.

"You're about my son's age, aren't you? Finished high school a couple years ago?"

"Year ago," I said.

He nodded. "It's nice to see such respect for a father."

I didn't know what he wanted me to say to this.

He was quiet a long time, standing there looking at the room. "Well," he said finally. "Tell your dad I think he does very handsome work."

"I will," I told him.

"It sure looks nice," he said.

"Hard work," I said.

He smiled. "New money."

"Right," I said. "New money." I couldn't believe it.

"What's wrong?" he said.

"Nothing. My father says that—new money."

"Oh, yeah. I don't know where that comes from."

"It comes from my father," I said.

He was thinking about something else. "Right," he said. "Well."

"That's the only place I ever heard it," I told him.

He looked at me with this expression like he might ask me for a favor. It was almost hangdog. "I hope you both realize what you have."

I said, "Oh, right."

Then we stood there looking at the room. It seemed like a long time.

"I'll let you get back to work," he said, and I headed away from him. "It's a nice job," he said. "An excellent job."

"People notice good work," I said. I was just mouthing it now.

"Your dad teach you that?"

"That's it," I told him. I thought something might break in my chest. I just wanted to know why he wouldn't get out of there and let me get on with the job. "That's what I

learned," I said. And for half a second I could see it in his
face, what he was thinking: how, between the two of us—
the man with the money to buy a big house like this, with
its wraparound porch and its ten-acre lot and the intercom
in the walls and three fireplaces and all the nice stuff that
was going to be moved into it soon—how, between that man
and me, I was the lucky one.

EQUITY

for Marjorie Allen

WHEN she'd sold the house in Charlottesville and given away or sold most of the furniture, Edith Allenby bought a condominium in Tampa, but after the first year she seldom stayed there. She claimed she missed the snow in Virginia, and she didn't have to say she missed her three daughters, Allison, Ellen and Carol.

And so for the last few years the pattern had been that she would visit them each in turn, staying a month or two, and then moving on to the next house. She had interrupted the pattern at various times when she considered that one daughter needed her more than the others, or when in her mind there was too much tension in a house for the added pressure of having a visitor. And since the middle daughter, Ellen, had recently undergone a painful divorce—after three children and in the third trimester of a late pregnancy— Edith had stayed for the better part of a year with her. She'd been present for the birth of the child, whose conception had been one of the breaking points in Ellen's marriage, her husband being unwilling or unable to take on the responsibility of another child so late in life. Edith was often on the telephone to the sisters during those months, and she told the youngest daughter, Carol, who lived in Washington, that coaching Lamaze was better than presiding over divorces and nervous troubles—meaning, of course, Carol's breakdown. Carol had reached the stage where she could call it that herself, and almost interrupted Edith to tell her so. Edith went on: "I've been through Allison's divorce, and your

little—thing. And now Ellen's divorce, and I've coached
Lamaze. How about that? Aren't I quite the doctor?"

"Yes," Carol said. "You are that, Mom."

"I mean about the Lamaze, sweetie."

"I know," Carol said.

"I wasn't talking about anything else."

"*Mother.*"

"All right, all right."

"How's Ellen doing?"

"Ellen."

"Mom."

"Oh, Ellen. Ellen's doing fine. The baby's fine. We're all
very happy."

"Mom," Carol said, "you are quite amazing to us all."

"Are you making fun?" Edith wanted to know.

Carol had been serious. And after they'd hung up, she sat
crying, thinking about Edith with the ridiculous hospital robe
on, standing in the lobby of the emergency room, yelling
into the phone.

WHEN the more obvious signs of her mother's illness began,
Carol spoke to a doctor friend, who told her there could have
been subtle indications of the trouble for several years: signs
that might've gone under the name of eccentricity or seemed
like quirks of personality, of the fact that she was aging and
might be expected to throw away some of her old inhibitions.
Carol thought immediately of Edith's habit of pilfering things
from one daughter's house and spiriting them into the next:
if she thought Ellen would appreciate a scarf that Carol wore,
she would steal the scarf during her stay with Carol and hide
it in Ellen's closet when she visited Ellen. Allison might
notice that a box of chocolates had disappeared at about the
same time that Edith was on her way to Carol's—and a week
later Carol, looking for something else, would discover the

box hidden in the seldom-used kitchen cabinet over the re-frigerator.

The three sisters, ranging in age from thirty-four (Carol) to fifty (Allison), had grown accustomed to finding each other's things in strange places, and were often inclined to wonder what might be lurking under a bed, or in the back of a closet, the bottom of a cedar chest. The joke between them had been that in order to set everything right, they would have to take a kind of inventory. And they had joked about it, as they'd joked about other habits of Edith's: her girlish love of Paul Newman at all the stages of his career; her fear of mice (she had nightmares about them); her love of chocolate; and the fact that, for all her apparent presumption in wishing to achieve some sort of equal distribution of her daughters' possessions, she still claimed to consider herself only a visitor in their houses, with no rights at all; she wouldn't allow anyone to treat her like a guest, and was always saying so.

"That's right, Mother," Ellen had said to her one Christmas, having opened a present from her which turned out to be a skirt Carol had given Allison on her birthday the previous March. "As long as you don't want us to treat you like a thief."

Edith hadn't understood the joke.

Perhaps this was the first time any of them realized that she couldn't help what she did any more than she could remember having done it.

LAST June, after almost exactly a year, she'd come to stay with Carol again, and had brought along a tin of hard candy that Carol learned had been in Ellen's pantry. Carol put it in a package and mailed it to her sister with a note in which she talked about their "communist" mother. But perhaps a week later she woke in the middle of the night to the smell of burning, and found Edith standing naked in the glare of the overhead light in the kitchen with a soup ladle in her hand, and an empty saucepan on the stove. The burner was on, and gas flames licked up the sides of the pan. It was as though she'd been sleepwalking.

"Mom?" Carol said.

Her mother seemed momentarily startled. But she said, "You go on, dear. I'll make us something scrumptious."

"Let's have it later," Carol said, and guided her gently back to bed.

The following morning, Edith had no memory of the event, and as she learned what happened all the color went out of her face. "I'm not a sleepwalker," she said. "What in the world." She sat staring, and Carol moved to her side, put her arm around the thin shoulders.

"Maybe you just got too tired," Carol said.

There had followed several sleepless nights, and perhaps the younger woman had noticed a certain increasing garrulousness in her mother, an unsettling forgetfulness. But there were no more sleepwalking episodes. When the visit was over and Edith headed south to Charlottesville, her daughter decided that it had all been the result of one of those small seizures she'd read about that the elderly were subject to— a ministroke, the effects of which were transitory. But she was unable to quite dismiss the one instance from her thoughts.

ALLISON and Ellen still lived in Charlottesville, in separate houses. Edith went to stay with Allison next, and it was while she was there, during the autumn, that things grew quickly much worse. Allison called Ellen or Carol almost daily with bad news. The doctors were describing with clinical efficiency what lay ahead, what would be required, and clearly matters concerning their mother were growing beyond them. Edith was getting worse all the time. She'd wander out of the house and be gone for hours; you had to go get her and bring her back. Twice recently she'd gone out alone in the predawn, walking the dark streets in a bathrobe, humming tunes to herself. She talked incessantly, and of course she'd always had stories to tell, but these were the same childhood tales over and over. The last time she'd gone roaming, the police had picked her up for shoplifting. "It's driving me crazy," Allison said to Carol over the hum of long distance. "My work is suffering, I have no private life anymore, I never know what to expect. I'd ask Ellen to take her, but you know what things are like for her now, with those kids and starting a new job at the university, and the older kids just aren't up to baby-sitting an old woman and a toddler, too. But something's got to be done, and quick, I'm telling you. Something decisive and rational."

"Should we get a nurse?" Carol said.

"I've got a nurse. I've been paying a nurse for two weeks now."

"Well what, then?"

"We want you to come to Charlottesville. Ellen wants to talk about it. We all have to agree on something."

"Allison, what are we talking about?"

"I don't know. We don't know. Really, Carol. Ellen just feels that whatever we do should be done together. That way the responsibility can be equally distributed."

"Responsibility."

"Please come," Allison said. "Please don't be difficult."

"Things aren't so good right now," Carol said.

"Explain."

"It's just going to be hard to do. How long are we talking about?"

"Are you having trouble again?"

"No, it's not that," Carol told her, and she couldn't keep the annoyance out of her voice.

"Well. What do *I* know," Allison said. "People do have relapses."

"How long are we talking about?" Carol said.

"We have to do some things, don't we? A couple days, anyway."

"When?" Carol said.

"Now. Tomorrow. The next day. You say. But soon."

"Thursday," Carol told her.

Two years ago, out of a kind of restlessness, she'd ended a long relationship with a man, someone who didn't matter at all now but whose absence, quite oddly, worked on her in ways she couldn't have supposed it would. She was bored with him; things were going nowhere, and so she broke off with him. She spent two days feeling free of the burden of having to work at everything, but then with the gradualness and the secret speed of clock hands a malaise had set in—a completely unexpected, pervasive sense of spiritual sickness which undermined her normally confident nature and left her in a state of almost suicidal despair. She stopped going out, stopped returning her mother's and her sisters' calls, saw no one, and time died out. Mornings blended into afternoons, into evenings. She quit her job by simply ceasing to go to it, and as the money she'd been saving all that summer began to go, she marked the diminishing balance of her checkbook as though it were the number of days she had to live.

Into this darkness Edith had come one Sunday, peering into the first-floor window of the apartment and saying her name. It was like all those days when she had been a little girl and Edith had called from another part of the house. Even so, she had no memory of letting her into the apartment. But Edith came in and sat down across from where she lay on the couch, and took Carol's hands into her own and looked at her. "Okay, now, Missy," she'd said. "Suppose you tell me what this is all about."

There was something in the commanding, matter-of-fact tone of her voice that made Carol calmer inside. The air seemed somehow charged and fragrant again, though there were soiled clothes everywhere. She looked into the sharp brown eyes and felt that her mother could do anything. "I don't know," she said.

"Of course you do," said Edith.

And Carol began to cry. It was the first thing she'd felt in perhaps six weeks. She cried and Edith gathered her into her arms.

"You just wait," Edith told her. "I'm going to fix you up. I'm going to *concentrate* on you, young lady."

"I'm okay," Carol said, because it was what people said in such circumstances. But she held tight to Edith's side.

"You know what, honey? You held on to me just like this when your father died."

Carol didn't remember much about it. She saw a room, a pair of shoes. There were people standing with their backs to her. She had dreamed these things; they were like something someone had told her.

"You went for days without saying a word to anybody and without showing the first sign of what you felt. You just pulled down into yourself and wouldn't come out for the world. Do you remember? We were all very worried about you, and then one morning you perked right up and asked me for pancakes."

Carol nestled and said nothing.

"Yes, ma'am," Edith said. "I'm going to get you right again, sweetie."

And for the weeks that led into winter, Edith worked on her, made her go out, squired her from place to place around the city, claiming that she wanted to be shown the nation's capital by someone who had lived there. She cooked and cleaned and talked and cajoled and teased, and one late evening she initiated the conversation—at a restaurant in Alexandria—with the young man who became friendly with both women and who, that spring, moved in with Carol, though Edith had gone to stay with Ellen by then and had no knowledge that things had progressed that far.

Which was somewhat of a complication now, since, last summer, during her mother's most recent visit, Carol had asked the man to sleep elsewhere rather than trouble Edith with the facts. His name was Ted, he was a college student, nine years younger than Carol. Because there had lately been a kind of uncertainty between them, she'd been purposefully vague about the trouble concerning her mother, and she wondered how she could speak of it at this late date.

Finally she couldn't do it.

There were more important things, and somehow it was a matter of pride that he not know how far her mother's decline had progressed. She kept the whole thing to herself through the week, and on Thursday morning she lay in bed pretending to sleep, watching him move around the room, readying himself for work. He was a dark, boy-thin man, full of suppressed angers about everything—the culture he found himself in; the failures of his family; his job; his schoolwork; his own inability to organize himself. Yet he could be charmingly self-deprecating and lighthearted when he wanted to be.

"Hey," he said.

She feigned drowsiness, yawned, extending her arms. "Hey."

"Aren't you going to get up?"

"Sure."

"I'll be late coming home today," he said. "I have to go to the library and do some work."

"Okay."

"I might go have some drinks afterward."

"Fine," she said. She lay there looking at him. The fact that she was going to be gone when he returned felt like some sort of advantage. And then she thought about this feeling and pulled the blankets up over her shoulder. She was suddenly chilly.

"You can come, too, if you want," he said. "You want me to call when I'm through?"

"If you want to."

"Do you *want* me to."

"Okay," she said. "Are you mad at me?"

"Why would I be mad at you?"

When he was gone, she called the savings bank where she now worked and took two days of sick leave. Once she'd begun to act she didn't think about him, or what he might say or do. The chill had left her. She packed a small overnight bag and one suitcase, and before she left, she wrote him a note.

Ted,
Sorry, had to go to C'ville. Will call you and explain.
Love, Me.

ALLISON'S house was near the University of Virginia campus, in a cul-de-sac of small three-bedroom ramblers which had been built just after the war and were now a little rundown and depressed-looking, with uniformly awninged windows and brittle hedges shedding leaves and brown, dirt-patch yards. Carol drove up to the house and Allison came out, carrying herself with the placid erectness of someone for whom such apparent calm has exacted a price. She kissed Carol on the side of the face, then spoke quietly, with all the quiet reverence of funerals: "Ellen's already left for the restaurant to make sure we get a table. You're late."

"Can I see Edith first?"

Allison seemed faintly exasperated.

"Is it all right?" Carol said.

Allison turned and led her inside. Edith sat in a straight-backed chair in the low-ceilinged living room, looking very much older. The bones of her face seemed swollen, as though they might break through the waxy smoothness of the skin. Some discoloration had set in around her mouth. A nurse Allison had hired was combing her hair. Allison herself was all business. Indeed, she was like Edith in better days: brilliant-eyed with will, her mind made up. "Ellen's at the restaurant," she said. "Let's not keep her waiting. There are kid requirements, remember."

Carol leaned down and looked into her mother's eyes. "Mom?" she said.

Edith stared at her and seemed momentarily perplexed.

"It's me," Carol said.

During those awkward weeks of last summer while her mother stayed with her, Ted had stopped by in the afternoons or called in the evenings, as he had in the first days of his acquaintance with them. The whole thing had taken on aspects of television comedy, with poor Ted trying to seem brotherly, uninterested in Carol as a sexual partner. He was a perfect gentleman. He took them out to eat and to the movies; he bought roses for Edith, and was positively gallant; and when Edith got on the train south, he punished Carol by disappearing for two days. He'd gone to get drunk, he said, and spent two nights in a miserable motel room alone. He was hurt. He'd started to think about what it meant that Carol was afraid for her mother to know what their true situation was. "Do you want to get married?" he'd said. "Is that it? You think I'm afraid? You think I won't marry a woman older than me? We'll get married."

Carol told him she did not want to get married.

"Mom?" she said now.

"Oh," said Edith, smiling at her. "Hello."

"Mom, it's me," said Carol. "Ted says to say hello."

"Of course it's you."

Carol kissed the cool forehead.

"I'm with Dorothy now," Edith said, and she turned to the nurse. "Dorothy, say hello."

"Hello," the nurse said.

"Let's go," Allison said. Then she touched the nurse's wrist. "We'll be back in a little while."

THERE had been fog and some misty rain in Washington, but over the miles of the journey the mist had dissipated and the day had taken on that vividness which makes October so beautiful in the mountains: cool, leaf-fragrant breezes, bright fall colors everywhere on show, and puffy canyons of cumulus, brilliantly white in the sun. Allison drove. The trees on either side of the street were almost bare, and the yellow leaves that littered the road surface swirled in the wind the car made. Carol looked at the black branches and thought of sickness.

At times last summer, Edith had called her by the name of a long-dead sister. They had joked about it. Carol had humored her by answering to the name. Twice Edith corrected herself. "Good Lord, you're not Dee. Why am I calling you Dee?"

"Do I look like Dee?" Carol wanted to know.

"Not even a little bit, honey."

"Maybe I remind you of Dee."

"No."

Carol had then turned it into a joke. "If you want to call me Dee, you call me Dee. How many names is a person supposed to remember in a lifetime?"

Now she recalled that she had felt so good then, a year removed from the darkness, better, healed, Edith's patient in full recovery, and Edith's small lapses had been a shadow on it all. Something she didn't want to think about. She turned to Allison and said, "I hate this."

"Don't judge," said her sister.

"*Judge.*"

"I don't want to talk about how awful things are," Allison said. "There's no sense pointing out the obvious."

"I'm not pointing out the obvious."

"Yes, you are. You always do. When you turned thirty-two you called me and bothered to point out that you'd reached the age Mom was when she had you. As if this were important and as if we didn't all know it."

"Okay," Carol said. "Maybe I'll try not to talk at all. You might remember that I'm the one who got to go through the death of her father at seven years old."

A moment later, Allison said, "I'm sorry, honey. Jesus, let's not argue."

The sidewalk which traversed the row of shops across from the Colonnade Club was crowded with couples in suede jackets and patched faded denims and cords; a group of runners crossed at the intersection, wearing suety-looking burgundy tights and metal-colored sneakers. Little knots of people stood on the corner decked out in outlandish jewels and beads, riotous decorations, wild colors and hairdos, as if a whole segment of the population had achieved rock stardom.

Here, on campus, everyone looked heartlessly young.

"What did Ted say about your coming down?" Allison said.

"I haven't talked to him about it yet."

"What did you do, leave him a note?"

"It's what you do when you simply don't have it in you to explain anymore. It seems like explaining is all we ever do these days."

"Oh, no," Allison said.

"Don't jump to any conclusions," said Carol.

Ellen was waiting for them on the sidewalk in front of the restaurant. She looked heavier, and Carol remembered that she had been having trouble with her diabetes. They hugged and cried a little, and Allison stood by. She would not be emotional now. She took Ellen's hand when Ellen offered it but did not move into the embrace. Allison taught school and was dating someone Ellen often teased about—a nervous, tentative man whose devotion to her seemed somehow forlorn, as though he were already certain she would leave him. In two years he hadn't worked up the courage to ask if they might live together, and Allison had decided to let him take his time. Things were comfortable. She was in control. Indeed, she had always seemed more confident than the others; it had been Allison whose decisions always appeared to come out of some deep well of self-assurance, and Carol had often supposed that it was a matter of strength, some gene of determination that had been passed down from Edith. One didn't think in terms of happiness, looking at Allison; one saw glimmers of emotion in her face: anger or disappointment or dismay or determination, or gladness; but there was always something else, too—something indefinably and profoundly still. A repose. In some obscure way, one always failed to attend to her laugh, and it was difficult to imagine that she ever allowed herself to falter or stumble into the areas of doubt that plagued her sisters.

"Come on," Ellen said, opening the door. "I've already got our table." They followed her through the dimness to a booth in a back corner. Menus large and unwieldy as posters had been set out in three places, and Carol, sitting across from the other two, thought of plates in rows on cafeteria tables, the food one gets in institutions. She saw Ellen looking at her. Poor Ellen, with her four children and her husband off in the western mountains, living with someone else, a client he'd met in his work as an architect. Horsewoman, the sisters called her.

But there was something in Ellen that invited abuse, and often enough Allison would pick on her—the province of the older sister, perhaps. Allison seemed to know what targets to hit, and when she was angry enough she never hesitated. The two older sisters had been feuding off and on ever since Carol could remember, and sometimes they went for weeks without speaking to each other. Usually it was Edith who brought them back—or bullied them into an alliance against her.

Carol thought about the fact that today they were in a different kind of alliance.

Before she sat down, Allison lit a cigarette and then went looking for an ashtray at another table. When she returned, she offered the others a cigarette.

"No," Ellen said, plainly annoyed. "How can you think of smoking with that cough you've had all fall?" Carol saw Allison decide not to respond, and they made themselves comfortable, as if this were an ordinary occasion. They didn't speak about Edith at first. The waiter came, and they ordered lunch, and then Ellen told a story about her three-year-old waiting for her rice to get cold and then trying to count it, grain by grain, when she couldn't get much past ten. When she asked Carol how the drive south had been, Carol talked a little about Highway 29, which seemed a foot or so narrower than all the other dual-lane roads in Virginia.

"Okay," Allison said suddenly. "I think we all know that we should put Mom in some kind of hospice or something."

"Hospice," Carol said. "Isn't that for the dying?"

"Oh, come on. What do you think is happening, anyway? Don't you know what the end of this is?"

They looked around the dim room at the other patrons, the pictures on the walls. The restaurant was relatively new, and predictably its clientele was mostly college students. The music coming from the walls was some vague, unpleasant hybrid of rock 'n' roll and disco. It was not loud enough to be more than faintly distracting, and even so Carol decided that she didn't like the place, with its splashy colors on the walls and its air of being campy and outrageous, as if the world existed purely for entertainment. The waiters were dressed like someone's idea of Hollywood in 1930. They wore pencil-thin mustaches and had their hair slicked down, and the lapels of their jackets were absurdly wide. She looked out the window and saw a man walking a little boy along the sidewalk. The little boy stopped to pick up a handful of red leaves and held them out to the man, and there was something in the open, uncomprehending, delighted expression on his small face that sent a shiver of grief through her.

She remembered her mother's old, morbid talk of dying, the casual way she'd always managed to bring it up—her insistence that no ceremony accompany her into eternity, since she couldn't stand the thought of people praying over her. The best thing was to be put away and out of sight, the sooner the better. And there were to be no measures to prolong her life, either, no medicines or treatments or discussions of treatments. Nothing could be worse than to be the subject of whispered conferences in hospital hallways—all those weighty deliberations over the dying, as it had been during her husband's last illness. "Just let me go when the time comes," she'd said many times. "No frills and no prayers. Just leave me my dignity."

Well, it was not going to be that simple now. And Edith was not going to have her dignity.

"God," Carol said, feeling as if for the first time what it meant to suffer the gradual disappearance of her mother. Perhaps in tiny, almost imperceptible increments the effacement had been going on for a long time, but the thought of it now in its steady, terrible progress was no less shocking, somehow: Edith, with her throaty laugh and her temper; her love of swing music, old musicals, painting and sculpture; her stubborn attention to her children, her profound interest in their lives as if there were improvements to be made, still work to do as a parent—that woman was already gone. "Do you remember," Carol said, "how Mom always hated the idea of people deliberating over her?"

"I know what you're going to say," Allison told her. "And you can spare yourself the energy."

"I was just going to say here we are, deliberating."

"I know what we're doing," Allison said, blowing smoke.

Carol said, "I wasn't trying to cause trouble."

"Nobody has to cause it, honey. It's here."

Ellen said, "Mom doesn't know we're deliberating, Carol. She's getting so she doesn't know anything at all."

"Oh, please," Carol said, "I don't think I'm up to this."

"We have to be," said Allison.

The waiter came and set their food down. Carol had ordered a hamburger, and the smell of it made her want to cover her mouth. She pushed the plate a little to the side and turned to look out the window again.

"Incidentally," Ellen said in a trembling voice, "I'm missing a bracelet."

Carol frowned at her. "This is not the time."

"I can't find a comb and brush set I was saving to give a friend of mine at school," Allison said.

"Stop it, both of you. I didn't drive all the way here for this sort of talk."

"All right, look," Allison said. "I called a couple of places. We can go tour them today."

And Carol said, "What if I take her back with me?" The sound of her own voice was a surprise to her. The others stared.

"We're past that sort of discussion," Allison said.

"Maybe I don't want us to be past it."

"Oh," Ellen said. "Don't start."

"I'm not starting anything. I just asked a question."

"It's the wrong question."

"Yes, but why? Why couldn't I take her? Couldn't we all go in together and hire a nurse? There's room."

"You can't be serious," Ellen said.

"I am," said Carol. "I am serious." She felt extremely good all of a sudden, as if something had opened out inside her. She put her hands down on the table and watched her sisters look at each other.

"Well," Allison said. "I just think that's crazy. She barely knows us anymore. Soon she isn't going to know us at all. I mean, she's going to need round-the-clock care, and her insurance will pay for professionals to do it. Qualified people."

"But what if I decide to take her?" Carol said.

"What about Ted? Could you get Ted to agree to a thing like that?"

"I don't want to talk about him," she told them and was surprised by the abrupt stir of anxiety which blew through her at the sound of his name. What if he were to read her note and simply move out? She thought of the apartment empty, his things gone from the closet, and she had to fight an urge to go call him, to leave this table and this discussion of another life, a life not her own, which had been so darkly threatened only a year ago. What if Ted had arranged to meet someone else at the library or the bar—someone closer to his own age, someone who shared his rage at the world's failure to acknowledge him or conform to his vision of it? Her sisters were talking, and she breathed, tried to listen. For some time she had been feeling uneasy, waiting for something to change, idly entertaining the idea that perhaps it would happen soon: perhaps he would leave; perhaps she would find herself on her own again. She had courted such thoughts, like daydreams about madness, and there had been a kind of thrill in it, because it provided a contrast; it was a way of looking upon how far she had come from trouble. And yet here was the deep shiver in her blood when she pictured him reading the note. When it occurred to her that he might actually leave. She remembered how it had been the last time—the sinking into darkness, the days of a kind of dank sleep, of a horrible quiet, and quite suddenly she knew she wouldn't be able to stand living alone. She had an image of herself in the rooms of the apartment with Edith, who would need her for utterly everything.

". . . and I'm in debt up to my eyeballs now," Allison was saying, "I haven't received a support payment in eight months. I can't afford it anymore. I just can't. And the insurance will pay if she's hospitalized. I mean, we've already been through this."

"You all have," Carol said, fighting back tears. In her distress it seemed to her that they had always kept her on the outside, and now they were going to turn away from Edith.

Both of them were protesting that they had kept Carol informed, and Allison put her hand on her arm. "We can't start recriminating with each other," she said.

Ellen said, "I feel like I should go home and start looking for things that don't belong to me," and put a napkin to her face.

"We can't sit around crying about it," Allison said. "It won't go away just because we wish it would."

Carol looked out the window again. The sun was everywhere, and everyone looked happy. Without wanting to, she was thinking through what she would say to Ted. It was important to be extremely careful. She would say that it was something she'd had to do, had to resolve, putting Edith in the hospital. She would tell him the call was sudden. There hadn't been time to do more than write the note. She wanted to call him now, and yet she sat very still, barely holding on, feeling the panic rise in her face and neck.

Her sisters were talking about how at one time or another each of them had felt as though Edith were shutting the others out to concentrate on her alone. It had been almost like a competition. "Well," Allison said "maybe it's because I'm the oldest, but even when she was being impossible and I was mad at her I liked being with her."

"I used to like talking to her about you guys," Ellen said. "Me, too."

"God, don't use the past tense about her," Carol said, too loudly. The panic had worked its way inside her bones, it seemed. Her own hands looked too white to her.

"I know we seem hard," Allison said. "But I'm thinking of our mother, too. I know what she'd want. And she doesn't want to be seen wandering the streets like a bag lady."

"You know what happened this summer?" Carol said, feeling vaguely petulant. "She called me Dee, and she told me she thought she'd failed with us."

"Are you all right?" Ellen said.

"I'm fine."

"Well, I guess she did fail with us," said Allison.

The others waited for her to go on, and when she didn't, Ellen said, "I've got four of them I'm failing with."

"At least you *have* children," said Allison.

"Would you like two of mine?"

Allison shrugged this off. "All right," she said. "We can go on record and say that it was all my idea. But I'm for choosing a place today."

"Not a hospice, though," Carol said.

"Carol," said Allison, suddenly. "Do you really think you could do it—you know, take over?"

They both looked at her. "Oh," she said, the dampness moving under her skin. "I—no. It's—you're right about it. It's impossible."

"All right, listen," Ellen said. "We have to do this together. We have to agree on it, and we have to find a place, and look at it and everything together. That's the only way." She bit into her sandwich and sat there chewing, looking almost satisfied, as though everything were accomplished. But then her expression changed. "It sounds like we're planning a murder, doesn't it?"

They were both looking at Carol. "Listen," she said. "I know I suggested it. But I can't take her. It's impossible, okay?"

"Calm down. No one expects you to do anything of the kind."

She found that she couldn't return their gaze. She stirred the coffee she hadn't drunk and tried not to think of Edith among strangers.

"When Mom arrived here this time," said Allison, "she gave me a blouse. I think it was the one I bought for you, Carol. Two Christmases ago. It was all wrapped up, and she'd sprayed something on it, some fragrance or other that I didn't recognize. But it was the same blouse." Her voice broke.

"I have a cake mold that belongs to somebody," Ellen said.

Carol excused herself and went to the ladies' room. She had to ask the hostess where it was—down a flight of stairs, past a row of closed utility doors and a wall telephone. The rest room itself was small, windowless, with a single mirror over the sink. The light was bad, and the flower design in the wallpaper had faded to the same brown shade. She stood in that closetlike space and was quiet, and then she cried into her hands. It all came over her like a fit, and she'd been wrong about everything. How badly she feared that her life might change. In her own eyes now she was what she was: someone clinging to small comfort, wary of the slightest tremor. She washed her face, fixed her mascara. It was a matter of facing up to realities. Certainly it was a matter of practical truth. Yet she felt trapped. As she left the rest room, she saw her own image in the wall mirror across the corridor, and it was like Edith's. Something in the smudges on the glass had given her face a darker, older look. Climbing the stairs, she thought of her mother spiriting objects from one house to another, and something occurred to her that seemed suddenly so right it stopped her: what if, all those years the sisters had looked with tolerance and with humor upon Edith's pilferage—talking of it as an attempt to force some sort of equal share of everything—what if it had been instead a kind of web her mother had meant to spin around and between them as a way to bind them together, even as she slipped away.

How awful to be so alone!

She reached the top of the stairs, shivering. Her sisters were waiting for her in the dim little corner beyond, and as she approached them she had a bad moment, like heartbreak, of seeing herself elsewhere, going through things her mother had wanted her to have from their houses; in her mind it was decades from now, a place far away, past the fear of madness and the dread of empty rooms—and she was an old woman, a thin, reedy presence with nervous hands rummaging in a box of belongings, unable to quite tell what was actually hers and what wasn't, what had been given and what received, with what words and by whom, and when.

LETTER
TO THE LADY
OF THE HOUSE

IT's exactly twenty minutes to midnight, on this the eve of my seventieth birthday, and I've decided to address you, for a change, in writing—odd as that might seem. I'm perfectly aware of how many years we've been together, even if I haven't been very good about remembering to commemorate certain dates, certain days of the year. I'm also perfectly aware of how you're going to take the fact that I'm doing this at all, so late at night, with everybody due to arrive tomorrow, and the house still unready. I haven't spent almost five decades with you without learning a few things about you that I can predict and describe with some accuracy, though I admit that, as you put it, lately we've been more like strangers than husband and wife. Well, so if we are like strangers, perhaps there are some things I can tell you that you won't have already figured out about the way I feel.

Tonight, we had another one of those long, silent evenings after an argument (remember?) over pepper. We had been bickering all day, really, but at dinner I put pepper on my potatoes and you said that about how I shouldn't have pepper because it always upsets my stomach. I bothered to remark that I used to eat chili peppers for breakfast and if I wanted to put plain old ordinary black pepper on my potatoes, as I had been doing for more than sixty years, that was my privilege. Writing this now, it sounds far more testy than I meant it, but that isn't really the point.

In any case, you chose to overlook my tone. You simply

said, "John, you were up all night the last time you had pepper with your dinner."

I said, "I was up all night because I ate green peppers. Not black pepper, but green peppers."

"A pepper is a pepper, isn't it?" you said. And then I started in on you. I got, as you call it, legal with you—pointing out that green peppers are not black pepper—and from there we moved on to an evening of mutual disregard for each other that ended with your decision to go to bed early. The grandchildren will make you tired, and there's still the house to do; you had every reason to want to get some rest, and yet I felt that you were also making a point of getting yourself out of proximity with me, leaving me to my displeasure, with another ridiculous argument settling between us like a fog.

So, after you went to bed, I got out the whiskey and started pouring drinks, and I had every intention of putting myself into a stupor. It was almost my birthday, after all, and—forgive this, it's the way I felt at the time—you had nagged me into an argument and then gone off to bed; the day had ended as so many of our days end now, and I felt, well, entitled. I had a few drinks, without any appreciable effect (though you might well see this letter as firm evidence to the contrary), and then I decided to do something to shake you up. I would leave. I'd make a lot of noise going out the door; I'd take a walk around the neighborhood and make you wonder where I could be. Perhaps I'd go check into a motel for the night. The thought even crossed my mind that I might leave you altogether. I admit that I entertained the thought, Marie. I saw our life together now as the day-to-day round of petty quarreling and tension that it's mostly been over the past couple of years or so, and I wanted out as sincerely as I ever wanted anything.

My God, I wanted an end to it, and I got up from my seat in front of the television and walked back down the hall to the entrance of our room to look at you. I suppose I hoped you'd still be awake so I could tell you of this momentous decision I felt I'd reached. And maybe you were awake: one of our oldest areas of contention being the noise I make— the feather-thin membrane of your sleep that I am always disturbing with my restlessness in the nights. All right. Assuming you were asleep and don't know that I stood in the doorway of our room, I will say that I stood there for perhaps five minutes, looking at you in the half-dark, the shape of your body under the blanket—you really did look like one of the girls when they were little and I used to stand in the doorway of their rooms; your illness last year made you so small again—and, as I said, I thought I had decided to leave you, for your peace as well as mine. I know you have gone to sleep crying, Marie. I know you've felt sorry about things and wished we could find some way to stop irritating each other so much.

Well, of course I didn't go anywhere. I came back to this room and drank more of the whiskey and watched television. It was like all the other nights. The shows came on and ended, and the whiskey began to wear off. There was a little rain shower. I had a moment of the shock of knowing I was seventy. After the rain ended, I did go outside for a few minutes. I stood on the sidewalk and looked at the house. The kids, with their kids, were on the road somewhere between their homes and here. I walked up to the end of the block and back, and a pleasant breeze blew and shook the drops out of the trees. My stomach was bothering me some, and maybe it was the pepper I'd put on my potatoes. It could just as well have been the whiskey. Anyway, as I came back to the house, I began to have the eerie feeling that I had reached the last night of my life. There was this small discomfort in my stomach, and no other physical pang or pain, and I am used to the small ills and side effects of my way of eating and drinking; yet I felt the sense of the end of things more strongly than I can describe. When I stood in the entrance of our room and looked at you again, wondering if I would make it through to the morning, I suddenly found myself trying to think what I would say to you if indeed this *were* the last time I would ever be able to speak to you. And I began to know I would write you this letter.

At least words in a letter aren't blurred by tone of voice, by the old aggravating sound of me talking to you. I began with this and with the idea that, after months of thinking about it, I would at last try to say something to you that wasn't colored by our disaffections. What I have to tell you must be explained in a rather roundabout way.

I've been thinking about my cousin Louise and her husband. When he died and she stayed with us last summer, something brought back to me what is really only the memory of a moment; yet it reached me, that moment, across more than fifty years. As you know, Louise is nine years older than I, and more like an older sister than a cousin. I must have told you at one time or another that I spent some weeks with her, back in 1933, when she was first married. The memory I'm talking about comes from that time, and what I have decided I have to tell you comes from that memory.

Father had been dead four years. We were all used to the fact that times were hard and that there was no man in the house, though I suppose I filled that role in some titular way. In any case, when Mother became ill there was the problem of us, her children. Though I was the oldest, I wasn't old enough to stay in the house alone, or to nurse her, either. My grandfather came up with the solution—and everybody went along with it—that I would go to Louise's for a time, and the two girls would go to stay with Grandfather. You'll remember that people did pretty much what that old man wanted them to do.

So we closed up the house, and I got on a train to Virginia. I was a few weeks shy of fourteen years old. I remember that I was not able to believe that anything truly bad would come of Mother's pleurisy, and was consequently glad of the opportunity it afforded me to travel the hundred miles south to Charlottesville, where cousin Louise had moved with her new husband only a month earlier, after her wedding. Because *we* traveled so much at the beginning, you never got to really know Charles when he was young—in 1933 he was a very tall, imposing fellow, with bright red hair and a graceful way of moving that always made me think of athletics, contests of skill. He had worked at the Navy Yard in Washington, and had been laid off in the first months of Roosevelt's New Deal. Louise was teaching in a day school in Charlottesville so they could make ends meet, and Charles was spending most of his time looking for work and fixing up the house. I had only met Charles once or twice before the wedding, but already I admired him and wanted to emulate him. The prospect of spending time in his house, of perhaps going fishing with him in the small streams of central Virginia, was all I thought about on the way down. And I remember that we did go fishing one weekend, that I wound up spending a lot of time with Charles, helping to paint the house and to run water lines under it for indoor plumbing. Oh, I had time with Louise, too—listening to her read from the books she wanted me to be interested in, walking with her around Charlottesville in the evenings and looking at the city as it was then. Or sitting on her small porch and talking about the family, Mother's stubborn illness, the children Louise saw every day at school. But what I want to tell you has to do with the very first day I was there.

I know you think I use far too much energy thinking about and pining away for the past, and I therefore know that I'm taking a risk by talking about this ancient history, and by trying to make you see it. But this all has to do with you and me, my dear, and our late inability to find ourselves in the same room together without bitterness and pain.

That summer, 1933, was unusually warm in Virginia, and the heat, along with my impatience to arrive, made the train almost unbearable. I think it was just past noon when it pulled into the station at Charlottesville, with me hanging out one of the windows, looking for Louise or Charles. It was Charles who had come to meet me. He stood in a crisp-looking seersucker suit, with a straw boater cocked at just the angle you'd expect a young, newly married man to wear a straw boater, even in the middle of economic disaster. I waved at him and he waved back, and I might've jumped out the window if the train had slowed even a little more than it had before it stopped in the shade of the platform. I made my way out, carrying the cloth bag my grandfather had given me for the trip—Mother had said through her rheum that I looked like a carpetbagger—and when I stepped down to shake hands with Charles I noticed that what I thought was a new suit was tattered at the ends of the sleeves.

"Well," he said. "Young John."

I smiled at him. I was perceptive enough to see that his cheerfulness was not entirely effortless. He was a man out of work, after all, and so in spite of himself there was worry in his face, the slightest shadow in an otherwise glad and proud countenance. We walked through the station to the street, and on up the steep hill to the house, which was a small clapboard structure, a cottage, really, with a porch at the end of a short sidewalk lined with flowers—they were marigolds, I think—and here was Louise, coming out of the house, her arms already stretched wide to embrace me. "Lord," she said. "I swear you've grown since the wedding, John." Charles took my bag and went inside.

"Let me look at you, young man," Louise said.

I stood for inspection. And as she looked me over I saw that her hair was pulled back, that a few strands of it had come loose, that it was brilliantly auburn in the sun. I suppose I was a little in love with her. She was grown, and married now. She was a part of what seemed a great mystery to me, even as I was about to enter it, and of course you remember how that feels, Marie, when one is on the verge of things—nearly adult, nearly old enough to fall in love. I looked at Louise's happy, flushed face, and felt a deep ache as she ushered me into her house. I wanted so to be older.

Inside, Charles had poured lemonade for us and was sitting in the easy chair by the fireplace, already sipping his. Louise wanted to show me the house and the backyard—which she had tilled and turned into a small vegetable garden—but she must've sensed how thirsty I was, and so she asked me to sit down and have a cool drink before she showed me the upstairs. Now, of course, looking back on it, I remember that those rooms she was so anxious to show me were meager indeed. They were not much bigger than closets, really, and the paint was faded and dull; the furniture she'd arranged so artfully was coming apart; the pictures she'd put on the walls were prints she'd cut out—magazine covers, mostly—and the curtains over the windows were the same ones that had hung in her childhood bedroom for twenty years. ("Recognize these?" she said with a deprecating smile.) Of course, the quality of her pride had nothing to do with the fineness—or lack of it—in these things, but in the fact that they belonged to her, and that she was a married lady in her own house.

On this day in July, in 1933, she and Charles were waiting for the delivery of a fan they had scrounged enough money to buy from Sears, through the catalogue. There were things they would rather have been doing, especially in this heat, and especially with me there. Monticello wasn't far away, the university was within walking distance, and without too much expense one could ride a taxi to one of the lakes nearby. They had hoped that the fan would arrive before I did, but since it hadn't, and since neither Louise nor Charles was willing to leave the other alone while traipsing off with me that day, there wasn't anything to do but wait around for it. Louise had opened the windows and shut the shades, and we sat in her small living room and drank the lemonade, fanning ourselves with folded parts of Charles's morning newspaper. From time to time an anemic breath of air would move the shades slightly, but then everything grew still again. Louise sat on the arm of Charles's chair, and I sat on the sofa. We talked about pleurisy and, I think, about the fact that Thomas Jefferson had invented the dumbwaiter, how the plumbing at Monticello was at least a century ahead of its time. Charles remarked that it was the spirit of invention that would make a man's career in these days. "That's what I'm aiming for, to be inventive in a job. No matter what it winds up being."

When the lemonade ran out, Louise got up and went into the kitchen to make some more. Charles and I talked about taking a weekend to go fishing. He leaned back in his chair and put his hands behind his head, looking satisfied. In the kitchen, Louise was chipping ice for our glasses, and she began singing something low, for her own pleasure, a barely audible lilting, and Charles and I sat listening. It occurred to me that I was very happy. I had the sense that soon I would be embarked on my own life, as Charles was, and that an attractive woman like Louise would be there with me. Charles yawned and said, "God, listen to that. Doesn't Louise have the loveliest voice?"

AND that's all I have from that day. I don't even know if the fan arrived later, and I have no clear memory of how we spent the rest of the afternoon and evening. I remember Louise singing a song, her husband leaning back in his chair, folding his hands behind his head, expressing his pleasure in his young wife's voice. I remember that I felt quite extraordinarily content just then. And that's all I remember.

But there are, of course, the things we both know: we know they moved to Colorado to be near Charles's parents; we know they never had any children; we know that Charles fell down a shaft at a construction site in the fall of 1957 and was hurt so badly that he never walked again. And I know that when she came to stay with us last summer she told me she'd learned to hate him, and not for what she'd had to help him do all those years. No, it started earlier and was deeper than that. She hadn't minded the care of him—the washing and feeding and all the numberless small tasks she had to perform each and every day, all day—she hadn't minded this. In fact, she thought there was something in her makeup that liked being needed so completely. The trouble was simply that whatever she had once loved in him she had stopped loving, and for many, many years before he died, she'd felt only suffocation when he was near enough to touch her, only irritation and anxiety when he spoke. She said all this, and then looked at me, her cousin, who had been fortunate enough to have children, and to be in love over time, and said, "John, how have you and Marie managed it?"

And what I wanted to tell you has to do with this fact— that while you and I had had one of our whispering arguments only moments before, I felt quite certain of the simple truth of the matter, which is that whatever our complications, we *have* managed to be in love over time.

"Louise," I said.

"People start out with such high hopes," she said, as if I wasn't there. She looked at me. "Don't they?"

"Yes," I said.

She seemed to consider this a moment. Then she said, "I wonder how it happens."

I said, "You ought to get some rest." Or something equally pointless and admonitory.

As she moved away from me, I had an image of Charles standing on the station platform in Charlottesville that sum-

mer, the straw boater set at its cocky angle. It was an image
I would see most of the rest of that night, and on many
another night since.

I CAN almost hear your voice as you point out that once
again I've managed to dwell too long on the memory of
something that's past and gone. The difference is that I'm
not grieving over the past now. I'm merely reporting a memory, so that you might understand what I'm about to say to
you.

The fact is, we aren't the people we were even then, just
a year ago. I know that. As I know things have been slowly
eroding between us for a very long time; we are a little tired
of each other, and there are annoyances and old scars that
won't be obliterated with a letter—even a long one written
in the middle of the night in desperate sincerity, under the
influence, admittedly, of a considerable portion of bourbon
whiskey, but nevertheless with the best intention and hope:
that you may know how, over the course of this night, I
came to the end of needing an explanation for our difficulty.
We have reached this—place. Everything we say seems
rather aggravatingly mindless and automatic, like something
one stranger might say to another in any of the thousand
circumstances where strangers are thrown together for a
time, and the silence begins to grow heavy on their minds,
and someone has to say something. Darling, we go so long
these days without having anything at all to do with each
other, and the children are arriving tomorrow, and once more
we'll be in the position of making all the gestures that give
them back their parents as they think their parents are, and
what I wanted to say to you, what came to me as I thought
about Louise and Charles on that day so long ago, when they
were young and so obviously glad of each other, and I looked
at them and knew it and was happy—what came to me was

that even the harsh things that happened to them, even the years of anger and silence, even the disappointment and the bitterness and the wanting not to be in the same room anymore, even all that must have been worth it for such loveliness. At least I am here, at seventy years old, hoping so. Tonight, I went back to our room again and stood gazing at you asleep, dreaming whatever you were dreaming, and I had a moment of thinking how we were always friends, too. Because what I wanted finally to say was that I remember well our own sweet times, our own old loveliness, and I would like to think that even if at the very beginning of our lives together I had somehow been shown that we would end up here, with this longing to be away from each other, this feeling of being trapped together, of being tied to each other in a way that makes us wish for other times, some other place—I would have known enough to accept it all freely for the chance at that love. And if I could, I would do it all again, Marie. All of it, even the sorrow. My sweet, my dear adversary. For everything that I remember.

—Fairfax/Broad Run, Virginia
1987–90

About the Author

Richard Bausch is the author of four novels—*Real Presence* (1980), *Take Me Back* (1981), *The Last Good Time* (1984), and *Mr. Field's Daughter* (1989)—and a previous collection of stories, *Spirits* (1987). His stories have appeared in *The Atlantic Monthly*, *The New Yorker*, *Esquire*, *Wig Wag*, *Best American Short Stories*, *O. Henry Prize Stories*, and *New Stories from the South*, and he has twice been nominated for the PEN/Faulkner Award in fiction. In 1988 and 1990 he won the National Magazine Award. He lives in Fauquier County, Virginia, with his wife, Karen, and their five children.